WILLA'S FAMOUS S'MORES

A long time ago back in LA, I made this with my—well, let's just say with some people I shared my life with. They're gone now, but I've always held tight to the special memories of making this recipe with them. I'm in Thunder Ridge now, a town full of caring people...and a sheriff who keeps challenging my heart. I'm not sure I'm ready to love again, but I am ready to share these homemade treats with you. PS: I'm letting you in on my closely guarded secret!

Ingredients:

4 graham crackers
2 marshmallows
2 chocolate squares
2 metal skewers
metal grill basket

1. Lightly warm the graham crackers and chocolate by placing them in a metal grill basket high over the flame. The secret is making the crackers soft. Like love, it's all about not getting broken!

2. Skewer the marshmallow and hold it far enough away that the flame is just teasing it. Be careful not to burn it.

3. Stack a graham cracker, chocolate square and marshmallow, and top with another cracker.

This recipe makes two, so share them with someone you love. Tell them Willa sent you.

—Willa

THE MEN OF THUNDER RIDGE:
Once you meet the men of this Oregon town, you may never want to leave!

Dear Reader,

In the valley below a snow-capped mountain called Thunder Ridge lies a small Oregon town with wooden sidewalks, a showy river and a handsome sheriff who loves the local baker. He watches over her, even though she doesn't know it.

Thunder Ridge is a fictional locale, but it's similar to the real Oregon town I lived in. I like the quote, "A friend knows the song of your heart and sings it to you when your memory fails." That's what the people in Thunder Ridge do—they help each other heal and learn to truly *live* again. After a personal tragedy, Willa forgot the song in her heart, and I could think of no better hero than Derek to sing it to her.

It's my hope their journey will make you smile a lot, cry a little and remember what it feels like to fall in love.

And don't forget: every day, you're writing the greatest story ever told—your own!

With love,

Wendy

Kiss Me, Sheriff!

Wendy Warren

ISBN-13: 978-0-373-62334-1

Kiss Me, Sheriff!

This edition published by arrangement with Harlequin Books S.A.

For questions and comments about the quality of this book, please contact us at CustomerService@Harlequin.com.

Printed in U.S.A.

Wendy Warren loves to write about ordinary people who find extraordinary love. Laughter, family and close-knit communities figure prominently, too. Her books have won two Romance Writers of America RITA® Awards and have been nominated for numerous others. She lives in the Pacific Northwest with human and nonhuman critters who don't read nearly as much as she'd like, but they sure do make her laugh and feel loved.

Books by Wendy Warren

Harlequin Special Edition

The Men of Thunder Ridge

His Surprise Son

Home Sweet Honeyford

Caleb's Bride
Something Unexpected
The Cowboy's Convenient Bride
Once More, At Midnight

Logan's Legacy Revisited

The Baby Bargain

Family Business

The Boss and Miss Baxter
Undercover Nanny
Making Babies
Dakota Bride

Silhouette Romance

The Oldest Virgin in Oakdale
The Drifter's Gift
Just Say I Do
Her Very Own Husband
Oh, Baby!
Romantics Anonymous
Mr. Wright

Visit the Author Profile page at Harlequin.com for more titles.

This book is dedicated to LaCorius Jenkins,
who is smart and kind, courageous and true, and
a bunch of other wonderful things. You inspire me.

"In a gentle way, you can shake the world."
—Mahatma Gandhi

Chapter One

For the folks who cared to rise early enough, 6:30 a.m. was as fine a time as any on Warm Springs Road in Thunder Ridge, Oregon. The twinkle lights that glowed steadily through the night were still on. The Valentine's Day Decorating Committee met companionably at The Pickle Jar Deli for an early breakfast and a lively debate about whether to hang cupids or giant red hearts from the corner street lamps. And, next door to the deli, Willa Holmes opened the doors to Something Sweet, the bakery she'd been managing for the past two months. Her morning regulars typically arrived shortly after she flipped the "Done for the Day" sign to the side that announced, "Yep, Open."

Now, at precisely 6:32 a.m., Willa was at work behind the counter.

"Can I tempt you with a fresh Danish this morning, Mrs. Wittenberg?" She smiled at the tiny woman whose white curls bobbed just above the top of the glass pastry case. "They're still warm from the oven."

Baking since 3:00 a.m., Willa appreciated the early start time of her new job. The wee hours of the morning used to be for sleep or, back when she was first married, for lovemaking, but now she found late night and early morning to be the most difficult parts of her day. There was too much quiet time to think. And to remember.

Having breads to proof, cookies to shape and food costs to calculate provided relief from the thoughts that kept her awake at night. Her only coworker in the morning was Norman Bluehorse, who was either fortyish or sixtyish—it was seriously hard to tell—and who worked with earbuds in place and spoke only when he needed to ask or to answer a direct question. A few years ago that might not have suited Willa, but these days she appreciated Norman's unspoken you-mind-your-business-and-I'll-mind-mine policy.

Short on sleep due to the early morning and a restless night, she tried not to yawn. Mrs. Wittenberg peered closely at her.

"Sweetheart," the older woman said, "I hope you don't mind my asking, but is your red hair natural? I'm thinking about having a makeover. I used to have beautiful long hair, too. It fell out during The Change. Did you bake anything new this morning?"

Actually I think of my hair as light auburn...yes, it's natural... Your hair is lovely as it is...the pomegranate-orange bread is new. Willa only had time to think her responses before Mrs. W moved on to a new question or comment. This was their ritual six mornings a week. Mrs. W chattered brightly, examined every potential selection in the pastry case, then chose the very same thing she'd chosen the day before and the day before that—two lemon cloud Danishes and one large molasses snap to go.

"I added a touch of ginger to the lemon clouds today," Willa told the older woman, whose pursed lips were carefully lined and filled with a creamy rose shade even at this hour of the morning. "I think you'll like them."

Mrs. Wittenberg wagged her prettily coiffed head. "I don't know, dear. I think possibly I should choose something different this morning. It's a very special day."

"Oh?" Before Willa could ask why, the door opened to admit her second customer of the morning. A zing of pure adrenaline shot through her veins with such force, she actually felt weak. While Mrs. W tapped her upper lip, trying to make a selection, Willa's attention turned to the six-foot-two-inch sheriff of Thunder Ridge.

She hadn't interacted in any meaningful way with Derek Neel for the past couple of months, except to greet him and fill his order in the morning. She'd seen him around town, too, of course—he was fairly hard to miss, patrolling Thunder Ridge's wood-planked sidewalks on foot, or making the rounds of the broad streets in his squad car. He didn't just work in town, he lived here. Two weeks ago, she'd bumped into him in the cereal aisle of Hank's Thunderbird Market on a Monday night at 9:00 p.m. Impossible to ignore each other when you were shoulder to shoulder, contemplating breakfast. He'd smiled easily, asked if she thought "instant triple berry oatmeal" sounded good and then tossed the box into his cart after she'd replied that, sure, it was worth a try (which had been a total lie, because instant oatmeal was an abomination of the real thing and never a good idea). While he'd strolled off, she had remained rooted to her spot in the aisle like the proverbial deer in headlights, her thoughts rushed and confused, her emotions in turmoil.

Fact: she and the handsome sheriff had almost... *almost*...gotten to know each other in the biblical sense on one crazy, ill-advised night two-and-a-half months ago. It had been one of those evenings when sitting with her own thoughts had seemed painful, practically impossible. She'd been filling in for a sick waitress at The Pickle Jar, next door, and when a couple of the other servers mentioned they were heading to the White Lightning Tavern for a beer and a burger, she'd invited herself along.

Derek had been there, dining with Izzy Lambert Thayer, who co-owned both The Pickle Jar, where Willa had worked as a server when she'd first arrived in town, and the bakery Something Sweet. Izzy's new husband, Nate, had arrived at one point, and when he and Izzy got up to dance to The Louisiana Lovers, a visiting country western band, Derek had approached Willa's table and asked her if she would mind dancing with someone likely to two-step all over her toes. His eyes had sparkled, his lips had curved in good-humored self-deprecation, his open palm had hovered, steady as a rock, in front of her. He had made it so easy for her to say yes. So easy to laugh as they'd danced (and he hadn't stepped on her toes once). Easy to walk out the door with him later that evening, and easy—shockingly easy—to forget everything but the feeling of strong arms wrapped around her back as he'd kissed her.

Now, as Derek stepped into line behind Mrs. Wittenberg, he filled the small bakery with his bigger-than-life presence, neat and handsome in a crisply ironed beige uniform, his thick black hair still damp from a shower. Charcoal eyes met hers.

Just to prove she didn't have a cool or sophisticated bone in her entire body, heat instantly filled Willa's face.

Ducking her head, she refocused on the woman in front of her. "So what's the special occasion, Mrs. Wittenberg?"

Blue eyes, pink cheeks, and the tiniest, straightest teeth Willa had ever seen, beamed with pleasure. "Mr. Wittenberg and I are celebrating our fiftieth anniversary today."

"Oh. Oh..." *Wow.* A stab of pure, unadulterated envy caught Willa off-guard. "That's—"

Amazing. A gift. A reminder that life does not deal equally with everyone.

"Wonderful. That's really, really wonderful. Are you celebrating with a party?"

"No, dear. Our children wanted to, but Mr. Wittenberg and I have decided on a quiet time at home. Just the two of us. We're going to take an early walk along the river. We got engaged there. This morning, we're going to visit the very same spot. There's a little rock shaped like a chair. I sat on it while Mr. Wittenberg got down on one knee and proposed."

It was impossible not to be swept along on the tide of Mrs. W's pleasure and anticipation.

"Are you going to reenact the proposal?" Willa grinned as Mrs. W nodded vigorously.

"That's the plan." She giggled like a little girl. "Afterward, we'll walk back home, have a leisurely breakfast... And then I'm going to take that man into the bedroom and seduce him."

Willa's smile froze on her face. Her gaze shot to the sheriff. He was watching her. One eyebrow, as midnight black as his hair, arched in devilish humor.

"Do you have something sexy I could serve?" Mrs. Wittenberg continued. "The Food Network says breakfast can be a potent aphrodisiac."

The mischief in the sheriff's expression flared to a broad grin. A very sexy broad grin.

Alrighty. Willa looked at the pastries she'd baked with fresh appreciation. Up until now, the most interesting question she'd fielded was, *Do you make gluten-free strudel?*

"A sexy breakfast, hmm?" she said. "I have a chocolate chip babka Mr. Wittenberg might enjoy." She pointed to a tall, dome-shaped breakfast bread filled to bursting with chopped chocolate and cinnamon sugar.

Mrs. Wittenberg eyed the coffee cake. “It looks good.” Her penciled brows knit together. “I don’t know if it’s sexy enough, though.” Turning, she enlisted the aid of Thunder Ridge’s finest. “Sheriff Neel, do you think a chocolate chip babka is sexy?”

Appearing to give the elderly woman’s question his serious consideration, he drawled, “I don’t watch too many cooking shows, Mrs. W, but I like to think I’m a fair judge of desirable. If the Food Network thinks you need an aphrodisiac, they’re underestimating your charms.” Because he towered above her by more than a foot, he had to bend down quite a bit to whisper loudly in her ear, “You’re already irresistible. Just think of the coffee cake as an appetizer.”

Turning back to Willa with a smile that seemed bigger than her face, Mrs. Wittenberg crowed, “I’ll take the babka! Can you put a bow on the box?”

“Of course.” Willa’s glance lighted on Sheriff Neel. He winked. Once again, heat filled her face. *Like I’m a teenager*, she thought disgustedly, giving herself a mental shake as she went about the business of wrapping the coffee cake.

Apparently Sheriff Neel was perfectly relaxed and comfortable continuing to have casual encounters with her after their episode of very heavy petting. It was, after all, the twenty-first century. Plus, there was no shortage of women in town who spoke frankly about their interest in bringing Thunder Ridge’s sheriff home for a night—or forever. What happened between him and Willa at the end of summer had probably happened to him a bunch of times.

Well, all except the part where Willa had pushed him away, exclaiming, “I can’t do this!” and then ran away as if the devil were on her heels. *That* had probably been a new experience for him.

"Here you are." Handing Mrs. Wittenberg a white box with red lettering and a glittery gold bow, she said, "I added a couple of molasses snaps. For later."

"Oh, thank you so much, dear. I'll let you know how it goes!" Showing her deep dimples, Mrs. Wittenberg hugged the box to her as she exited the store.

Which left Willa alone with her next customer.

It was too quiet, too still in the bakery. Willa made a mental note to ask her boss if she could play some music during the day. Even the large fan that pulled heat out of the kitchen sounded like nothing more than a faint hum.

Derek didn't seem bothered by the stillness. He was pretty still himself, watching her, waiting patiently. He had sought her out the day after their near miss, looking concerned rather than angry. He'd asked her why she'd run away, of course, and hadn't been satisfied with her insistence that she'd simply been having a bad night, had thought a little socializing might do her some good, but hadn't meant to let things go that far.

He'd frowned, staring at her, waiting for a fuller explanation, and she'd felt so guilty, because he was a good guy. When she'd waitressed at The Pickle Jar, she'd seen him nearly every day. Her employer, Izzy Thayer, was his best friend, and he'd come in regularly to have a cup of coffee, do some minor repairs or keep a very wary eye on the progress of Izzy's relationship with Nate Thayer before Nate and Izzy married. Derek just seemed like a natural protector, and that was nice. *Very* nice. But Willa had learned there were some things from which no human power could protect you.

So she'd stuck to her guns, claiming that what had happened between them was a mistake and wouldn't happen again. "I'm very, very sorry for the..." She'd stumbled, not knowing what to say. "For leading you to believe I was..." *Ugh.* "I mean, if I led you on in any way." She was *so* not cut out for dating.

With the sexy, easy smile that was his trademark, he'd stood on the front porch of her rented cottage and shrugged away her apology. "No harm done. I just wanted to make sure you're okay."

"Me? I am." She'd nodded vigorously, as if being emphatic would turn her lie into the truth. She hadn't been "okay" in two years. But that had nothing to do with him.

Now, this morning, he transferred his gaze from her to the pastry case. "Got anything to tempt *me*?"

The words didn't sound utterly innocent, but his tone did, so she took them at face value. Reaching into the case, she withdrew a large flaky golden rectangle.

"Our signature cheese Danish," she said.

He squinted at the glazed pastry. "Where's the cheese?"

"Inside. It's filled with a blend of ricotta, cream cheese and honey. And a touch of orange zest and cinnamon."

"A Danish with hidden charms." He nodded. "Okay, I'll try it. And a large black coffee." Withdrawing his wallet, he pulled out a few bills. "I'm going to need the caffeine to stay extra alert now that I know Mrs. W's plans." He looked at Willa with a straight face, but roguish eyes so darkly brown they appeared black. "Mr. Wittenberg is ten years older than his wife, you know. If that babka really is an aphrodisiac, he may not survive the morning. I hope I don't have to bring you in for aiding and abetting an aggravated manslaughter."

The comment made Willa smile, and she remembered that he'd made her smile quite a lot, actually, that night in the tavern. "It isn't my recipe," she countered, "so I don't think I should be held responsible." She shrugged. "On the other hand, forewarned is forearmed, so thanks. I'll go home at lunch and pack a duffle bag in case I have to run from the law." She turned, the curve of his lips an enjoyable image to hold on to as she got him a large coffee to go and slid the Danish into a bag.

Derek paid her, the expression in his eyes that mesmerizing combo of sincere and humorous. "I hope you won't run from the law. I'm here to help." He gave her a quick nod. "Morning."

She watched him go, sharing a few words with an older gentleman who walked in as he walked out.

"Good morning, Mr. Stroud," Willa greeted the new arrival as he approached the counter. "Toasted bialy and cream cheese?" She named the savory round roll he had every morning. Soon, Jerry Ellison, who owned First Strike Realty up the block, arrived and sat with Charlie Stroud at one of the six small tables in the bakery. Business picked up the closer they got to 7:00 a.m., and Willa stayed busy throughout the morning.

"I'm here to help."

A couple of hours after Derek left, his parting words continued to play through her mind. She'd heard those words, or a variation of them, before.

"Don't try to do this on your own."

"You've been through so much. Let us help."

Didn't people know that their help was sometimes the cruelest of gifts? What they really wanted was to help her "move on," to "let go," to be happy again the way she used to be. To forget. And she couldn't let that happen.

"I don't want help. I don't need help," she muttered to herself as she slid a fresh tray of oatmeal chocolate-chip cookies into the oven. Kim Appel, a mother of young children who worked from nine to three or seven at the bakery, depending on whether her husband was available to pick the kids up from school, was now behind the counter while Willa toiled in the kitchen. That gave Willa plenty of time alone to obsess.

Her mind raced, her heart pumped too hard, her stomach churned. What was the matter with her?

"You're tired and you need some sleep, that's what." Wiping her perspiring palms on her apron, she gathered up bowls and utensils to stack them in the dishwasher. Maybe she should go home for a couple of hours. Kim could handle it; she was a capable worker. Willa could come back after a nap and close up shop.

Yeah, except whom was she kidding? She wasn't going to sleep. She was going to hear Derek's words over and over, see his sincere face, imagine his strong arms.

"I'm here to help."

For nearly a year now she'd caught him watching her and had sensed all along that he was interested. Interested in a way that, in a vulnerable moment, could make her skin tingle and her veins flood with heat.

He'd been unfailingly polite, courteous, gentle—never pushy—almost as if he sensed he would have to move softly if he hoped to get anywhere with her at all. And that agonizing yearning to lose herself in his arms, to forget for a night, for an hour…that yearning would sometimes overtake her like it had in the tavern. Her heart would race, and she would imagine surrendering to his arms and to his smile, to the unbridled laughter of lovers.

She would sometimes dream of *really* moving on.

Willa set the timer on the oven so she wouldn't burn the cookies while she cleaned the marble countertop. She hadn't moved to Thunder Ridge, eight hundred miles from family, friends and a brilliant career as a chef and culinary arts instructor so that she could forget everything. No. She'd moved so that she could live the way she wanted to—quietly, privately. She'd moved so she could hang on to the one thing that still held her broken heart together: her memories.

So far, she saw no reason to change.

When Derek walked through the door to the sheriff's office at seven-twenty, the sun was still trying to make its first appearance of the morning. The lights inside the large boxy room, however, were burning and emitted a warm, welcoming glow completely at odds with the rubber band that whizzed past his head with such force it could surely be classified a lethal weapon. Rearing back, Derek tightened his hold on the coffee cup, popping open the plastic lid and sloshing hot coffee over his hand and onto the linoleum floor.

"Russell," he growled.

"Sorry!"

Derek's deputy, Russell Annen, whipped his feet off the wide desk in front of him and stood. "I was aiming for Bat Masterson." He jerked his thumb at a poster of Old West sheriffs on the wall opposite him as he ran to fetch paper towels and sop up the spill.

"I hope you aim a gun better than you shoot rubber bands." Derek had almost had his eye put out on several occasions by Russell's wayward shots. "Slow night?"

"Yup." Russell bent to clean the mess. "Slow morning, too."

"You might as well take off then."

"I have another forty-five minutes."

"That's okay. You can get an early start." Heading for his desk, Derek noted the remains of Russell's breakfast littering the blotter: a liter bottle of soda and an open, half-eaten box of chocolate-covered donut holes. "Get a blood panel, would ya, Russell?" he suggested. "Check your sugar and cholesterol levels."

His deputy grinned. "Hey, I have to get my fix somewhere. LeeAnn watched some video about diet and heart disease, and now all she makes when I come over is vegetables and beans."

"Smart woman. You should marry her."

"I hate beans. Before that video, we used to look for the best burger-and-brew pubs. Now when we go to Portland, she wants to find vegan restaurants. Do I look like I'm meant to be vegan?"

Derek eyed his six-foot-tall, two-hundred-pound deputy. "You do not."

Russell began to wander toward their work area instead of toward the door, and Derek felt his shoulders tense. Seating himself behind the big oak desk, he pretended to become engrossed in his computer screen. Every morning after seeing Willa at the bakery, he required a few minutes alone to debrief himself. Willa took up residence in his thoughts more than anyone or, lately, anything else. It took some effort to refocus, and he liked to do that in private. His love life—or current lack of one—was his business, no one else's.

On that note, he said pointedly before Russell could sit down, "Enjoy your time off."

"I was planning to." Russell sighed heavily. "Before."

Do not, I repeat, do not take the bait. But Russell looked like a giant puppy whose favorite chew toy was stolen. *Give me patience.* "Okay." Derek crossed his forearms on the desk. "Before what?"

Closing the distance between himself and the desk, Russell dropped into the chair opposite Derek's. "See, it's this way. I made reservations for dinner up at Summit Lodge. Tonight. Their special is prime rib." He practically moaned the end of the sentence. "Eleven o'clock last night, LeeAnn tells me her cousin is in town today through the end of the week."

"So?"

"So, LeeAnn is refusing to go anywhere unless Penelope has something to do, too. And, someone to do it with."

"Can't she find something to do on her own?"

Russell slapped his palm on the desktop. "Dude, right? That's what I said. But Penelope and LeeAnn are females, see? They don't think like us."

Derek waited for more. "Okay. And?"

"So the only way I can go out with LeeAnn this week is if we double date."

It took a couple of seconds—only a couple—to understand. "No." Laughing humorlessly, Derek shook his head. "No way."

"It would just be for a couple of dates."

Picking up what was left of the coffee he'd brought over from the bakery, Derek leaned back so that his chair tilted on two legs. "No."

"Three dates, tops."

The front chair legs landed on the floor again with a thud. "Maybe you don't know this about me, Russell. I don't go on blind dates. Ever." He took a sip of coffee. "Good luck. I'm sure you'll find someone."

"LeeAnn thinks you and Penelope—"

"Someone *else*."

Blowing his breath out in frustration, Russell stood. "Fine." He turned and took several steps toward the door. Derek began to relax, but obviously everything was not fine, because Russell turned back. "It's not that you turn down blind dates. You don't date *at all*."

Narrowing his eyes, Derek warned, "Russell—"

"Not since that night at The White Lightning when you left with the woman who works at the bakery—"

"—you should go *now.*"

"I saw how you looked when you left with her. Everyone saw it. LeeAnn gave me holy hell for a week after that, wanting to know why I didn't look at *her* that way."

Derek was on his feet before he realized it. He didn't even remember putting down his coffee. *Laugh it off,* he advised himself, but he didn't feel very humorous. Covering his eyes, he took a deep breath and dragged his hand over his face. "What is your point?"

"I expected you to tell me you went to Vegas that night and got married by Elvis. But ever since then, you act like a monk. You wouldn't talk about what happened with her, but it obviously didn't work out, so why not go out with someone else? Why not Penelope? LeeAnn says she's fun, and she's not even vegan. I asked."

Derek looked down at the desk. His feelings for Willa baffled even him; the last thing he wanted to do this morning was attempt to explain them to somebody else. "I'm going to make a pot of coffee now, while you get going." He glanced up again. "If you don't, *I* may decide to take a few days off and put you on extra shifts."

The phone rang before either of them could say anything more, and Derek snatched it up. He listened for a bit, said, "Don't do anything. I'll be there in ten minutes," and hung up. "Jerry Ellison's potbellied pig knocked down Ron Raybold's fence again," he told Russell, "and Ron is threatening to shoot it and have a luau. I'm heading out."

Resignedly following his boss to the door, Russell asked, "Jerry is single, isn't he?"

"Yeah."

"When you talk to him, ask if he wants to go out with Penelope."

While Russell headed to his car, Derek put the "On a call… Back later" sign on the front door and went to forestall a neighborhood feud. Being the sheriff of Thunder Ridge was nine parts relationship mediation and one part active police duties. Truth was, most of the time he wouldn't have it any other way. He might not have been born here, but he'd found a home for the first time in this place where, rogue pot-bellied pigs aside, people cared about each other's business mostly because they cared about each other.

His life was good, and he hadn't thought much was missing until Willa Holmes had moved to town.

While Derek drove to Ron's place, he thought about the woman who had made him break one of his cardinal rules: no high-speed chases where women were concerned. If a woman didn't want to be caught, MOVE ON.

Like any lesson that made a lasting impression, he'd learned that one the hard way. Maybe it was the curse of having raised himself until he was nineteen, but for a while he'd pursued unavailable women. An attempt, he supposed, to prove to himself that he could make someone stay. He'd sworn off that kind of bull a long time ago.

Until Willa.

When he was near her, his heart revved like a car with the accelerator pressed to the floor. She'd turned away after what had to be some of the best kissing he'd ever experienced. No, *the* best. And he knew she'd felt it, too, because when he let himself think about it, he could still feel her fingers clinging tightly to his shoulders…then moving like smoke up the back of his neck…threading through his hair… The longer they'd kissed, the more her body had melted into his, and the more his had felt as if it were about to burst into flame.

Just when he'd been certain he was experiencing the

best moment of his life, Willa had cut and run. No real explanation given. Ever since then, he'd been on a high-speed chase all right, one with no end in sight.

But something in those mesmerizing eyes of hers, eyes with all the storminess and all the sunshine of a spring day in Oregon, told him to keep chasing. That she needed him to catch up even if she didn't know it yet.

Was he nuts? Behaving exactly as he'd sworn he wouldn't? Yeah. And he figured there were only two logical outcomes. Either he was someday going to become the luckiest man on earth, or he would realize he'd been the jackass of the century. He only hoped he could handle the fallout if the latter turned out to be the truth.

Chapter Two

"You sure you want to stay and close by yourself?" Kim looked at her manager with worried brown eyes yet not a line or a pucker on her silken brow, which reminded Willa how young her assistant was.

"I'm sure," she said. "Go home to your kiddos. The sun's actually out. If you hurry, you might have an hour left to get them outside before the stir-crazies set in."

"You're right." Kim laughed. "Three and six are probably the worst ages when you have to stay inside because of the weather and dark nights. They fight like crazy."

"Go on then." Willa shooed her employee toward the door. "Put on their mittens and let 'em duke it out at the park. Play structures are a mother's best friend."

As Kim left, Willa returned to work. She hadn't gone home after all, though she had taken a long lunch and had driven to Long River to go for a walk with other lunch-timers taking advantage of the unseasonably sunny winter day. Now, at 4:00 p.m., she was tired, but the more exhausted she was, the better her chances of sleeping tonight.

She began the process of wrapping up the leftover goodies in the pastry case so she could take them next door to the deli. Izzy would sell what she could tonight at half price, and tomorrow Willa would take the rest to Thunder Ridge Long-term Care for the staff and residents to enjoy.

The after-school crowd had already come in and cleaned her out of the most popular cookie selections, but there were still apricot rugelach, buttery shortbread and chocolate chip mandelbrot. The folks who would come in before closing would be interested mostly in bread, rolls and cakes for the evening meal, so she started packaging the cookies first. As Willa worked she flicked on the radio, opting for an oldies station, and didn't see her next customer come in until he was standing directly in front of the counter.

"Oh!" Using her upper arm to brush a stray hair from her eyes, she smiled. "Hello. You're here at a good time. All the cookies, bagels and rolls are two for the price of one."

The boy—ten or eleven, she guessed—pressed his lips together in a sort of smile and nodded. He wore a dark blue coat, pilling on the body and sleeves, and a knit hat that had also seen better days. His skin was a beautiful caramel color, his eyes as dark as onyx. He looked shy, and she couldn't recall seeing him before, either in the bakery or the deli.

"Do you like chocolate?" she asked.

He nodded, and she handed him a brownie. "Try that. On the house. Then you can look around and see if you want another one of those or something else."

He stared at her without moving. She nodded encouragingly. "Go ahead, take it. It's good. I like to think of it as a cross between a truffle and a brownie. Maybe I should call it a bruffle. Or trownie." He didn't smile.

"Free?" His only word to her was soft, a little suspicious.

"Yep. Bakeries give out samples all the time." Gingerly, he accepted the treat. "I'll be over there—" Willa pointed to the counter behind her "—working. If you decide to get something else, just holler. We have hot cocoa and cider, too, on the house in the evening." Beverages weren't really on the house, but what the heck? She'd drop a dollar fifty into the till. Sensing that her observation was making the boy nervous, she turned her back, slipping more cookies into the plastic bags she would deliver next door.

Something Sweet's grand opening had been in September, and Izzy had already orchestrated Dough for Dollars and other promotions with the local schools, plus there had been a back-to-school special the first two weeks the bakery had been operational. Now, every afternoon they had several kids from the local K-8 and high school stopping by for snacks, but she'd never seen this kiddo before. She'd have remembered him. His shy, almost distrusting demeanor stood in stark contrast to a face that was exotically beautiful.

Everyone, children included, had a story. What was his? As her curiosity grew, Willa shook her head. His story wasn't her business; she was just here to provide sticky sweets that temporarily soothed the soul and gave people a reason to brush their teeth. That's what she'd wanted when she had first come to Thunder Ridge—a simple job with work she could leave at the "office."

Several minutes had gone by when Willa realized she hadn't heard a sound from her young customer. Glancing over her shoulder, she saw him hovering near a large plastic canister she kept on the low counter near the cash register. There was a slit cut into the top of the lid and a big picture glued to the front and covered with tape to protect the photo. *"Help Gia."* Gia was fifteen and had lived at the Thunder Ridge Long-Term Care facility for the past ten months, after an auto accident that had taken her mother's life and left her father with ever-mounting medical bills and lost workdays. Thankfully, the canister was stuffed with bills and coins. Every Friday, Willa deposited the contents into a bank account set up for Gia and her family.

The boy had eaten his brownie and was frowning at the jar. He looked anxious, conflicted. Was he thinking about donating his money instead of buying something?

A sweet, sharp pang squeezed Willa's chest. Wow. People his age rarely gave the jar more than a passing glance. She understood that. It was so much easier to pretend bad things didn't happen to average kids. But maybe this boy was one of the unusually empathetic ones. She was going to give this cool kid a box of cookies and a hot chocolate if he dropped even a penny in that canister.

When he looked up and caught her watching him, she smiled. He appeared startled. Completely self-conscious. You know what? She was going to give him a box of cookies and a hot cocoa just for *thinking* about—

"Hey!"

Like a lightning strike, his hands were around the canister, pulling it beneath his coat. He turned and ran for the door with such speed, Willa was still standing in shock when the door harp pinged behind him.

For a second, she merely stared. Then outrage, pure and robust, rose inside her like a geyser. Gia's family needed that money. They needed the support it represented. They needed to know they were not forgotten, that *Gia* was not forgotten as she lay in a hospital bed in a long-term care facility.

Veins filling with adrenaline, Willa abandoned her post at the bakery, running full throttle after the boy. Twilight had turned to dusk, and the sunny day had given way to clouds that inhibited her visibility, but she caught sight of him up ahead.

To avoid running into a family, the kid dodged right, which forced him to skirt around a bench and slowed him down.

"Stop! You stop right now!" Willa hollered. Pedestrians turned to stare. Briefly, the boy looked back at her, too, his eyes wide. Then he jumped over a dog tied up to a street lamp and kept running.

Sophie Turner, who owned A Step in Time New and Vintage Shoes, was outside sweeping her front entrance when Willa raced by. "Willa?" the young woman exclaimed. "What's wrong?"

"He took my canister," she panted. "I've got to get him."

"He took…what? Do you need help?" Sophie called after her.

"No!" She cupped her hands around her mouth. "I'm warning you, you little twerp!" Really, she had been so wrong about this kid. "Stop. Right. Now!"

"Who are we chasing?"

Willa glanced to her right to see Derek Neel, out of uniform, jogging beside her. For a second, she was discombobulated. She'd seen him in street clothes before, of course, but tonight off duty Sheriff Neel seemed taller, more rugged and somehow relaxed even as he ran with her.

"He stole my donation jar," she said, panting.

"Who?"

"That kid!" Pointing, she accused, "That tricky little—Wait a minute, where'd he go?" Her eyes searched the darkening streets, but all she could see were a few scattered citizens of Thunder Ridge watching their sheriff and Willa run down the block together. "Darn it!" She stumbled to a stop, her breath heavy, her skin at once hot from exertion and cold from the thirty-five-degree evening. Suddenly, not even adrenaline could make her forget how tired she was, and how frustrated. "You made me lose him," she said, putting her hands on her thighs and bending over to catch her breath. "He's got all the money we've been collecting for a week. Do you know what that represented?"

"I'm not even sure what you're talking about." Derek's characteristic unruffled demeanor was intended to defuse the situation, but it had the opposite effect on Willa when he asked, "Who do you think took your jar?"

"I don't *think* he took it. I *know* he did." Her sudden fury at the kid was out of proportion, but she didn't care. "I was standing right there."

"Okay. And you say he looked like a kid."

"He didn't *look* like a kid. He *is* a kid." She started walking again, searching up and down the side streets, exasperated. "A kid with someone else's donation money."

"Okay, look, why don't you come on back to my office. You can give me a description, tell me what happened and how much money you think he's got."

"No." The word emerged too sharp, so she added, "Thank you. I'm going to find him."

Derek reached for her arm. "It's getting dark. He could have ducked into his house by now."

"Then I'll go door to door." Turning on Ponderosa Avenue toward the residential area, she strode up the block, searching. When she felt tears at the corners of her eyes, she swiped them away and kept walking. Derek stayed by her side, keeping pace until they had gone two blocks. Then he reached for her arm again, refusing to let go when she tried to pull away.

Because she was over-the-top, clearly, and probably irrational and maybe even a little scary, he looked at her in concern. "What is this really about?" His eyes searched hers as if he was trying to read what she wouldn't tell him.

She felt grief and fury rise inside her like dirty flood water. *I thought I was past this. I thought I'd cut this part of me out.* A couple of years ago, blinding anger had sprouted inside her as if it were a new organ. She'd worked hard to excise it, but tonight she felt as if she could scream—loudly and long enough to punch a hole in the night sky.

It had nothing to do with Derek. He was simply the hapless boulder standing in the path of her raging river. Willa's mind was on Gia—unable to speak clearly since the accident, barely able to walk and only fifteen. And her father, her poor father, probably felt responsible and utterly helpless.

Traumatic brain injuries were cruel. She'd wanted so much to show him his family was remembered every day.

"Never mind." She turned toward Warm Springs Road. She would get a new jar tomorrow, refill it herself and take it to the care facility. That, of course, was the reasonable solution. The boy was not her business. She shouldn't have interacted with him so much to begin with.

It took a moment to realize Derek was still holding her arm.

"I have to go. I left the store unattended." Which was a pretty stupid thing to do and an even dumber thing to admit to the owner's best friend. Great. Crazy Woman Loses Job would probably be the headline on the next *Thunder Ridge Gazette*.

"Okay, let's go."

"What? No. You were probably headed somewhere, and I'm fine. Really. I was over-the-top. Sorry." How many times could you apologize to someone for erratic behavior? "It was a long day. I'm fine now." She forced a smile. "Not crazy."

He didn't bother to answer. Didn't let go of her arm, either. With his jaw set in *capable sheriff mode*, he accompanied her back toward Warm Springs Road, Thunder Ridge's main street.

For future reference, Willa thought, *never tell someone you're not crazy. It makes you sound crazy.*

When they passed A Step In Time on their way back to the bakery, Sophie, who was young and pretty and single, ran to the door and smiled when she saw Derek. "Hi! Did you help Willa find her thief?"

"No, no need." Willa tried to sound philosophical. "He was just a kid. I lost perspective there for a few minutes. It's over and done now."

Beneath the street lamps that had switched on and the glow from the exterior light at Sophie's store, it was easy to see her brows pucker beneath a mop of caramel-brown curls. "I don't have kids, but if I did, I'd want to make sure they were held responsible for stealing. That boy's parents should hear about it." She divided her glance between Derek and Willa. "I hope you guys follow through."

"We will." Derek responded firmly. "Good night."

On they walked until they reached Something Sweet. Standing before the glass door, with the shop aglow inside, Willa hoped she would find the cash register exactly as she'd left it and figured she probably would. Crime was a relatively rare occurrence in Thunder Ridge. Before she opened the door, she said, "Everything looks fine." What were the odds she could persuade him not to come in? She needed some time alone to collect herself. "Thanks for walking back with me. I appreciate your help. I have some work to do and then I have to close, and I've taken enough of your time, so—"

"You're going to need to give a statement and a description of the suspect."

"No. I overreacted. Frankly, I'm embarrassed. Can we just forget it?"

Derek frowned. Disapprovingly. "This is about the boy now. I need to talk to his parents."

"Sure. Of course. It's pretty clear you aren't on duty right now, though." Her gaze traveled over his off duty attire—well-fitting black jeans and a zipped-up gray hoodie—and she wondered if he was meeting someone. A man that handsome, after all… Changing her train of thought, she offered, "So maybe I can swing by the station later tonight and talk to whoever's on call."

Derek reached around her for the door. He held it open and waited.

Quickly assessing the outcome of making an even bigger deal about this than she already had, Willa brushed past him. She didn't bother to walk behind the counter or into the kitchen. He wasn't going to leave, so she turned to face him in the middle of the bakery. Beneath the hoodie, she spied the top of a black turtleneck sweater that was exactly the shade of the thick waves that fell across his forehead. Yep, he definitely looked like a man with better things to do than solve the puzzle of her lunatic behavior.

"It seems I keep owing you apologies."

Raising one shoulder in a brief shrug, he said, "Nah. I'm not big on apologies. An explanation about what happened out there would be nice, though."

God knew she owed him one, but it would entail too many personal revelations, so she shrugged, too, hoping irony would diffuse the situation. "I'm not big on explanations."

"That's a problem then," he said. Hooking his thumbs

in his back pockets, he narrowed his gaze. "How do you feel about baos?"

"About what?"

"Baos. They're Chinese dumplings filled with meat. Sometimes beans."

"I know what they are." She'd once taught a class on Asian fusion cuisine.

"Good. How about eating some with me?" he invited. "Have you ever been to The Twin Dragon in Zig Zag? Best baos this side of Shanghai."

"Have you been to Shanghai?"

"Only in my dreams."

"Well, maybe someday you'll really go," she murmured. She *had* been to China. It had been a wonderful trip.

"I've been waiting for the right time," Derek said.

Her head rose at that. "You shouldn't. If you want to travel, you should just do it. Don't wait."

He gazed at her curiously, and she realized she'd sounded emphatic. "I'll take that under advisement," he said. He gestured toward the street beyond the window. "It's a big world out there. I'd like to see it with someone. That enhances the view, don't you think?"

"Yes." Uncomfortably aware that she hadn't responded to his dinner invitation, she clasped her hands in front of her. "I'd really rather not pursue finding that boy," she said, glancing everywhere but at Derek. "I think he was just… impulsive. I don't think he's a criminal."

"He'll be impulsive again."

"Still—"

"I'm not going to send him to juvenile hall. I want to talk to him and to his family. See if they're aware of what he's up to. Assuming he's never done something like this before, I'd like to make sure he doesn't do it again."

Reasonable. Derek was being very reasonable. She

couldn't argue without explaining her reluctance. "All right. After I close up here, I'll go over to your office to file a report and then head home."

The arch of his brow, the flare of awareness in his eyes and the near-imperceptible quirk at the corners of his masculine lips told her he got the message. No baos; just business. And no explanations, either.

"My deputy, Russell, is on duty all night. I'll text and let him know he should expect you."

She wanted to assure him that her rejection of his dinner invitation was not personal, but he was already on his way to the door. His broad, relaxed shoulders gave no indication that his feelings were wounded. Pausing with his hand on the door handle, he turned to consider her. "Maybe I should have been a detective. I like puzzles. Here's one I'm working on— beautiful woman—young, intelligent, capable of running her own business—moves to a small town in Oregon where she didn't know anybody and doesn't seem to want to. She takes a job working as a waitress in a deli. What would her motivation be?"

"For taking a job as a waitress? That's a rather elitist attitude."

"You have to consider the question in context," he said pleasantly enough. "The woman is clearly overqualified."

"Maybe she thought waitressing would turn out to be an upwardly mobile position."

"Could be." He nodded. "I doubt she would have assumed that at the start, though. There was no evidence that it would be."

"Well, it's hardly a mystery. Plenty of people move to Oregon because they want less stress and a pretty place to live. As for not socializing constantly, some people are naturally introverts."

"Maybe." Derek considered her for a long time. "Then again, maybe she's afraid."

"Of what?" Willa shook her head. "Never mind." She wagged her finger, trying to keep the moment light. "This is annoying, Sheriff. You're talking about me in the third person."

"I apologize. I had to repeat Language Arts in high school. Let me try it again. When I look at you, Willa, I see someone who wants to reach out, but won't. Or can't. I see something behind your eyes. Something you want to say or do, but wouldn't dare. And I can't help but wonder what it is. And why it's so hard." He opened the door, admitting a blast of cold air, and gave her one last look. "I'm not the enemy."

With that, Derek headed out onto the streets that were his to serve and protect.

Willa remained alone in the shop, shivering even after the door closed. The image of his searching dark eyes lasted long after he had disappeared.

Chapter Three

"You need to leave my employee alone, let her concentrate on her work, and go find a woman who actually wants you, because right now you are barking up the wrong tree." Izzy took a bite out of her pastrami and coleslaw on rye then spoke with her mouth full. "Gosh, I hope that didn't sound harsh."

"Gosh, it did." Derek unwrapped the deli sandwich Izzy had brought him. Once a week when the weather was decent, and often when it wasn't, he and Izzy met in Doc Howard Memorial Park. She supplied lunch from the deli, he supplied the appetite, and they sat by the river, talked and ate. Today he wasn't in the mood for food. "Is there mustard on this?"

"Of course."

"What about mayo?"

"Derek, please—" she sounded offended "—you've been eating the same sandwich for—what?—ten years? I know how you like it, and I respect your condiment selections." She poked at her own mammoth concoction, adding, "Even though I think they're misguided."

Brisket on challah had been his go-to sandwich since he'd had his first meal at The Pickle Jar. He liked it with mayo, spicy mustard, and—Izzy's main objection—ketchup.

"Since I can see that you are not ready to stop obsessing about the manager of my bakery, let's return to our regularly scheduled programming." Extending her legs and crossing her ankles, Izzy flexed her feet inside fuzzy faux fur–lined boots. "Recap. Willa turned you down for baos, which is too bad, but at least you asked, which is progress over last year when you were so afraid to be rejected you barely spoke to her."

"I was not afraid to be rejected. What the—" Sitting up straight, he glared at his best friend. "I didn't want to pressure her or put us both in an uncomfortable situation."

"Ooh. Good thinking, Dr. Phil."

"I didn't want to come off like a stalker. Okay?"

"Mmm. And now?"

"Now it's different. At the tavern, I saw that she *is* interested."

Lowering her sandwich, Izzy gazed at him, her sparkling eyes turning serious and more sensitive. "Derek, was she interested in *you*? Or was she interested in, you know, a man in general?" Obviously trying not to hurt him or to see him hurt himself, she rushed on. "Willa has been alone here for over a year. She doesn't really socialize with anyone at work. Maybe she's lonely and it was just…time." Placing a hand on his arm, she said, "I wouldn't hurt you for all the world, you know that. I know how much you have to give, and I want to see you happy. You said you weren't going to date unavailable women, anymore. Remember? You said you were going to be sane about your relationships. Unlike me." She grinned.

She can afford to grin about it, Derek thought, gratitude for his friend's happiness softening his mood somewhat. On Izzy's left ring finger were an engagement ring, the wedding band Nate Thayer knew he should have given her fourteen years earlier and an eternity band to signify Nate's commitment never to leave her again.

To say Derek had disliked Izzy's now-husband when he'd first met the man...well, that was an understatement. Nate Thayer had hurt Izzy once, before Izzy and Derek had met. After hearing the story and being Izzy's best friend for all these years, Derek had given Nate as hard a time as he could when the other man had shown up again, suddenly, last year. But Nate had turned out to be a good guy—hard to intimidate, too—and Izzy was nuts about him. Eventually, despite the trust issues born from his own past, Derek had given the pair his blessing, and they seemed to be doing fine. Great, in fact.

So, yeah, Izzy could afford to smile about it all now.

"That night in the tavern," he said slowly, looking at the river, "I sensed from Willa what I've been feeling all along. *Some* of what I've been feeling," he amended, figuring honestly that Willa wasn't as invested as he. "It was more than physical."

Izzy shook her head. "Even after a year of working together, I hardly know anything about her, beyond the fact that she has a strong work ethic and is completely reliable." She reached for a dill pickle. "You know, if I got a dollar every time someone asked me to set you up with them—or with their daughter or their cousin or their cousin's daughter's cousin—over the years, I could retire. So why this woman, this time? I mean, yes, she's lovely and I know you've had the hots for her, but, really, why Willa?"

The stretch of Long River where they sat flowed quietly, with little fanfare, but it was beautiful, mysterious and multifaceted as any white water Derek had ever seen. It reminded him of Willa. Her silvery eyes were soft, keenly observant, kind, sad—it all depended on the hour and the day. He could study her endlessly and still not see everything he knew there was to see.

"When we were in the tavern, I told her a joke. A really silly one."

"One of Henry's?"

"Yeah." Izzy's former boss, Henry Bernstein, used to offer his customers "A joke and a pickle for only a nickel." Derek had heard plenty of them (and had eaten a lot of pickles) over the years. "Willa liked it. She laughed. Really laughed. For the first time, her smile was in her eyes, too, and I could see..." He held up a hand as Izzy gaped at him. "Don't say anything. No wisecracks." He waited until Izzy nodded before he continued. "I could see what the future might be with her. And, yeah, there was something kind of desperate about the way she was behaving, but for a moment there, I think she was wondering what a future might be like, too." Izzy was looking at him seriously, as seriously as she ever had. He took a deep breath. "My gut's been telling me for a long time that this is different. This is special. So even when I took her home, I knew we weren't going to do anything more than kiss."

Izzy's brows rose to new heights. Stretching his own legs out toward the water, Derek shrugged. "I *might* have taken some upper body privileges. But that's it. When we—" He stopped. Too much information. But as he stared at the river, he let his mind float and thought, *I want Willa for more than a night.*

"You don't know much about her. Nobody does. There

isn't a lot of information to be found apparently. A lot of people have Googled her," Izzy confided.

"What?"

"Yeah. Come on, you haven't?"

"No." Not that he hadn't been tempted, but… "No. Someday she'll tell me what I need to know."

"Okay, well we mere mortals are curious right now. And you know what we found out?"

"No. And don't—"

"Almost nothing. There isn't much information to be found. Isn't that weird in this day and age? No Facebook, no Instagram—"

"I don't have that stuff, either—"

"—and while I support her desire to stay off social media, you have to admit that it's weird not to be able to find her somewhere online. These days, you can get a history of addresses for people who've lived under rocks—"

"That's an invasion of privacy. That kind of information should only be available for legal purposes."

"—and there are, apparently, over nine hundred Willa Holmeses, but none of them jump out as our Willa Holmes."

Derek told himself there was nothing unusual about someone living under the radar of the internet.

"Some folks are saying she's running away from a bad relationship," Izzy continued. "Marcy Anneting thinks Willa is in the Witness Protection Program, but Marcy belongs to a mystery book club. And Jett Schulman says you can tell by her manner that she was born into a life of luxury and is just here temporarily to see how the other half lives."

"When did you become the town crier, Izzy?"

He saw the sting of his words as her eyes flickered, but she didn't back down. "Since my best friend started to fall for a woman I don't think will ever love him back."

Unmindful of the sandwich she was squeezing tightly in her hand, Izzy exhaled noisily. "I don't think she *can* love you back. I don't know what the truth is. Maybe she was a mafia wife or her high school sweetheart died tragically and she can't get over it, or she's just a very normal, exceptionally private woman who is emotionally closed off. Whatever it is, she's not the woman I want for you. Derek, everyone thinks of you as having it all together, and you do. *Now.* But I've known you since you since you were the original rebel without a cause. We come from the same place, you and I."

"That was a long time ago. When I left my uncle's house, I didn't even know what I was running from."

"I think you were trying to run *to* something. Just like me. You've been searching for a loving family that was all yours ever since I met you. I don't want you to be hurt again."

"And you think one small, shy woman can do that?" He smiled, hoping to tease Izzy out of her concern, but she refused to be distracted.

"I think she could, yes. I want to protect you, because I love you. Like you tried to protect me when Nate came back."

"Yeah, and I was wrong," he pointed out. "Everything turned out all right. Better than all right."

She stared at him a long time then slowly wrapped the remainder of her now squished sandwich and put it in the insulated lunchbox she'd brought with her. "Okay."

"Izz, I love you. But I've got to go with my gut on this."

She wouldn't look at him. "Yeah. Well, I hired her, you know? I brought her into our lives, so I guess I feel responsible."

He chucked her on the chin. "Okay, you can be the best man at our wedding." When she swiped at a tear, he realized how serious she was and felt a pinch of surprise. But he'd already considered all the possibilities. He knew where he was headed, and he wasn't changing direction. "Izz, I know this may turn out to be nothing. I do. I accept that. I'll deal with it."

She sniffled. "You want to get married. You want a family."

"Yeah," he admitted. "I've borrowed yours long enough."

She pulled back. "Derek! Don't even say that."

He smiled. "Hey, you and Eli are stuck with me." For the past ten years, he'd spent nearly every holiday, every birthday and plenty of days off with Izzy and her son, who was now fifteen and getting to know his father for the first time. Eli didn't need "Uncle Derek" constantly in the way. "I'm ready to branch out, that's all. Widen the circle a bit."

"Okay, I get it, but you *are* family, and my being with Nate doesn't change that." Izzy spoke emphatically, even though she'd said it all before.

She still couldn't accept that the past Thanksgiving and Christmas had been different. On this first holiday as a family, Nate would have preferred to keep his wife and his son all to himself. It had been obvious, no matter how Nate had attempted to mask the feeling. Derek would have felt the same.

He rose. "I should get back to the station. Russell thinks he has the flu, so I'm on duty the rest of the day and night. I'll take the sandwich with me."

"Yeah, I need to get going, too. We ordered Pickle Jar hoodies for Thunder Ridge Community Church's Souper Bowl. I have to pick them up. I got you a hoodie, by the way. You're still going to serve soup with us, right?"

"Right. But if the hoodie has a giant dancing kosher dill on the front, I'm not wearing it." Izzy busied herself with reassembling the lunchbox. Her silence confirmed that the design was the same as on the T-shirts they'd worn for the Hood-to-Coast Relay last summer. He shook his head. "What is it with you and pickle promos? First it was the giant foam costume and now shirts with vegetables."

"The name of the deli is The Pickle Jar. Obviously, we need to promote. Besides, in case you haven't heard, pickles are hip. Don't be surprised if they turn out to be the staple snack food of the twenty-first century." When Derek started to laugh, she socked him in the arm. "I'm serious. And the shirts are terrific. The pickles aren't dancing this time. They have a cartoon face with a pickle mustache and the caption Got Pickles? Isn't that great?"

He looked at her in disbelief. "I'm not wearing that."

"Yes, you are." Izzy reached for her backpack then looked beyond Derek and frowned. "What are those kids doing?"

Derek turned. Beneath a madrone tree about a hundred yards away, two boys, one a teen and the other a bit younger, appeared to be engaged in some sort of transaction with money changing hands. It was a school day; neither of them should have been in the park to begin with.

Keeping his gaze on the duo, Derek uttered, "See you later, Izz," and started walking. About halfway over, he saw the smaller boy glance at him. Their eyes met. In one hand, the boy held a wad of bills he was about to pass to the teenager. As soon as he registered that the man walking toward him was an officer, his expression filled with trepidation. Before Derek could call out a word, both kids were off and running.

Adrenaline flooded Derek's system. Making a split-second decision, he took off after the younger boy, his feet pounding the grass, sure this was going to be anything but another ordinary afternoon in Thunder Ridge.

Can U come back to bakery? Sorry to ask, but it's important. Thx. Izzy.

Ordinarily her boss's text would not have frustrated her, but Willa hadn't slept at all the night before. She'd come home after her confrontation with Derek Neel and had done the worst thing she could do before trying to sleep, the very thing she had promised herself she would *stop* doing, in fact. She had watched a series of DVDs, each one labeled simply with her last name and the year the video had been shot. She kept them stored separately from the remainder of her modest DVD collection, and she never shared them with anybody else. They were hers and hers alone.

She'd finally fallen asleep around midnight, after plowing through half a box of tissues and taking two aspirin for the headache that followed her crying jag. The alarm had gone off at 2:30 a.m. and, after pressing the snooze button as many times as the clock allowed, she'd dragged herself into the shower and over to the bakery to begin work at three-thirty. It had taken an entire pot of coffee to push her along until noon today, which was when she'd cried uncle and headed home again.

Before Izzy's text, Willa had done one load of laundry, eaten two sticks of string cheese and a banana and, at 2:30—p.m. this time—she was wondering if she'd completely throw herself off by taking a nap. And then her phone had pinged. She often went back to work without any prompting from her boss, but this afternoon she thought she might fall over just thinking about returning to the bakery.

Sure. Be there in a few, she texted back. At least she'd be closer to her regular bedtime when she came home again. Maybe tonight would be merciful, and she would fall asleep easily and stay asleep until morning.

She'd already changed out of her flour-dusted jeans and into a pair of soft plaid lounging pants, a gray thermal top and her thickest socks. Piled into a half ponytail/half bun, her hair was no longer work-ready, but she really, really, *really* did not have the energy to get herself dressed and coiffed again. So for the first time since she'd gotten her job in Thunder Ridge, she stuffed her feet into boots, grabbed her coat and headed to work looking, she figured, like a soccer mom with a hangover.

Willa shoved her hands into the pockets of her coat and ducked her head against the chilly wind that had kicked up. As she neared Warm Springs Road, the main street through Thunder Ridge, she raised her head to nod at the locals who greeted her. It was easier to remain private, she had discovered, if she smiled and seemed happy.

She arrived at Something Sweet hoping to be done in record time with whatever business Izzy wanted to discuss. Noting quickly that the store seemed to be doing a brisk late business, Willa opened the glass door and scanned the room for her boss.

"Willa!" Izzy called. She was seated at the table nearest the kitchen. All four chairs were taken.

Rats. Instantly, Willa felt dizzy with fatigue. Multiple-person meetings often meant sitting through a sales pitch about some brilliant new mixer or a better brand of bread flour. Willa honestly didn't know if she could remain upright for that today. And then she focused long enough to recognize someone else at the table.

Derek. Sitting with his back ramrod straight, hands resting on his thighs, he was looking, not at her for once, but at the people seated opposite him. One was a dark-haired man in his twenties and one was a boy.

"Thanks for coming." Izzy got up and motioned Willa to the seat she'd just left.

Derek took a moment to nod at her, but kept his attention mostly on the young man and the boy seated with them at the table. The young man was scowling and turned his glare on Willa as she sat. The boy refused to glance her way at all.

"Sheriff Neel asked me to call you," Izzy explained, standing beside the table, "since you were the one who saw the donation jar being stolen."

"Thanks for coming in." Derek nodded at her. "Gilberto—" he gestured to the boy "—admits to taking the donation jar. Unfortunately, the money has already changed hands. Gilberto was using it to purchase a bike. When I ran after him, the teen selling the bike took off in another direction. So far, Gilberto doesn't want to give me the name of the other boy."

"You better give it." The younger man leaned across the table, his dark eyes flashing dangerously. "You want to go down for some jerk who left you to face a cop on your own? You're bringing disrespect to your family, Gilberto. You better pick who you're going to be loyal to, and pick fast."

Willa saw Derek's chest rise on a deep inhalation.

The boy cringed. *You're bringing disrespect to your family.* So the boy and the man were related. It seemed obvious now. They both had latte-colored skin, black hair, dark eyes and similar features. The resemblance stopped there, however. Gilberto had a shy, nervous demeanor; by contrast, his relative wore resentment and belligerence like a second skin.

"I'm telling you, Gilberto, if you bring any more trouble

home, I'm going to—" Cutting himself off, he thumped his balled fist against the table.

Derek's entire body tensed.

Like a puppy trying to evade his master's anger, Gilberto kept his eyes averted. He blinked several times rapidly. Willa recognized that expression: a child trying desperately not to cry in public. A child in pain.

"Excuse me," she said to the man, "I didn't catch your name."

"Roddy."

"Roddy. And are you Gilberto's…father?"

"Hell, no! That would make me, like, fifteen when he was born. I been more careful than that." He pointed between Gilberto and himself. "We're blood, so anything anybody's got to say goes through me. If he stole from you, *I* deal with it."

"If he stole, the *law* will deal with it, Mr. Lopez," Derek interjected, his voice calm, but every muscle in his body rigid. "What is your relationship *exactly*?"

"He's my cousin. I can take care of him."

Derek nodded slowly. "I appreciate your taking responsibility and asking Gilberto to do the same, but the law is involved now. We'll be keeping our eye on the situation. The *whole* situation."

"What's that mean?"

"Just what I said. Our interest in Gilberto will continue."

Derek was giving the man a clear message that abuse would not be tolerated. But Mr. Lopez was a bully, and Willa knew Derek wouldn't be able to intervene in their daily lives. More sadness washed through her. *Not your business. Stick to your own business.* She looked at Gilberto. "He didn't steal from me. He looks a lot like the boy who was in here yesterday, but…it's not him."

Gilberto's surprise was palpable. Derek looked at her. "He nodded when I asked if he took the donation jar."

"He's not the one."

Derek turned back to the boy. "Why did you nod?" he asked.

Evading everyone's gaze, Gilberto shrugged.

It was clear the men were about to cross-examine him. "Maybe he was afraid," she offered, "and thought things would be easier if he told you what you wanted to hear."

"Is that what happened?" Derek questioned.

Gilberto shrugged again.

Roddy smacked his hands on his thighs and slid low in his seat, tossing back his head. "Aw! Are you crazy? You lied to get *into* trouble. Cops love stupid suspects like you." He looked at Derek. "No offense, man."

Derek stared long enough to make Roddy sit up in his seat. "None taken." Then he turned his attention back to Gilberto. The next obvious question was *Where did you get the money you were exchanging for the bike?* but Derek didn't ask it. After a moment, he rose. "Make sure you're in school when you're supposed to be. I'll be checking with your teacher and the principal. Don't make me come look for you."

Gilberto nodded. He looked miserable still, but relieved and more than a little surprised. Was it over?

Willa supposed she was excused from the meeting and pushed back her chair.

"Walk me to the door, Ms. Holmes." In an official tone, Derek commanded rather than asked for her compliance.

Izzy appeared bemused by the entire exchange and simply shook her head. "I'm heading back to the deli. I'm sorry for the confusion, Mr. Lopez. Please feel free to order something on the house." Walking around them all, Izzy was the first out the door, followed swiftly by Roddy, who pushed Gilberto along in front of him, saying they'd take a rain check on the free snacks.

Now that her burst of adrenaline was spent, Willa felt exhausted all over again and proceeded heavily to the exit. Every movement felt like a Herculean effort. Raising his arm over her, Derek held the door while she passed through. Willa burrowed into her jacket, as she stepped onto a rain-sprinkled sidewalk. By tacit agreement, they walked several paces past the bakery then stopped.

"Thanks for going to the station last night to give the description of the boy who stole the money." Not bothered by the cold or the rain, Derek towered above her, six foot plus of straight-backed sheriff. "And for coming back to the bakery this afternoon. I thought it might be easier for everyone if we handled it away from my office. You know, still official, but less intimidating. I anticipated that would make it easier to figure out where we would go from here to help Gilberto."

Willa felt Derek studying her, but she kept her tired gaze on the street, watching the occasional car roll past.

"What I didn't figure on," he continued, "was walking away with mud on my face. I didn't figure on *you*."

She glanced up to see the first hint of anger she'd ever noticed him directing toward her.

Resting both hands on his gun belt, he shook his head. "I'm a good judge of people. In my line of work, you have to be. But this time, I blew it. I never, ever judged you to be a liar."

Chapter Four

"A liar?"

Fire-engine red filled Willa's body, flared in her face. She wouldn't be surprised if the color poured in jets of steam from her ears. *He was calling her a liar?*

Okay, she *had* lied. But the reason ought to be obvious.

Her fists were stuffed into the pockets of her thin coat. Pulling one hand out, she jabbed a finger toward the end of the street and stormed off, rounding the corner, not stopping until she reached the alley. "How dare you?" Her voice shook. "I told you I didn't want to get involved in this, but you had to keep pushing. If you could take no for an answer, there wouldn't be a problem."

The implication of her words hit them both at the same time. He hadn't accepted her "no" regarding Gilberto, and he hadn't accepted her "no" regarding the two of them.

Derek's face grew stormier. "The problem was already here. If you think anything else, you're being naïve."

Was he talking about Gilberto now or her? Willa pointed toward the bakery. "That man—Roddy," she said. "He was going to make that poor kid's life a nightmare."

"That 'poor kid' is going to make his own life a nightmare if he meets his needs by stealing. Roddy talks big, but he has a record, too. Petty crime is a family affair."

"I'm sure there are ways to help Gilberto that don't involve the law, exactly. His school—"

"'The law' is a set of boundaries designed to establish and maintain order. That's exactly what Gilberto needs and exactly what he's not going to get if bleeding hearts make excuses for him."

"Bleeding hearts! I can't believe you said that." Willa shook her head as if to dislodge his words from her brain. "Life does not respect rules and regulations. Life just happens, and it doesn't ask your permission before it gets messy, although that might be hard for you to accept, Sheriff. I've seen the way you run around town, trying to convince people we're all characters in a nineteen fifties TV sitcom."

"What are you talking about?" The words emerged muffled as Derek's jaw and lips barely moved.

"I'm talking about your town meetings and visits to the chamber of commerce and all the other places you go to tell people that as long as they do the right thing, they'll stay safe and happy and the world will be a better place, now let's all go have donuts. The end."

"I'm sorry you dislike the message that playing by the rules does make the world safer and better. I've found it to be true."

"Lucky you."

Derek's entire manner was different from anything she had seen before. His body looked stiff enough to break, and Willa sensed she should stop talking, just let it go, but he was so *sure* of himself, so smug about the world and how it worked, and she couldn't stay quiet. Especially since he'd called her a bleeding heart. "If you think Gilberto is going to have a better life because I rat him out to his bully of a cousin, then *you're* the one who's naïve, not me."

There were no lights in the alley, save for porch lights above the back doors of the businesses along Warm Springs Road, but Willa could see Derek's expression—closed and distant—and knew he could see hers.

In the chilly night, her breath came in small, visible puffs. She didn't feel cold, though. Her face and hands felt hot enough to fry eggs.

It wasn't like her to confront and criticize. She wished he'd say something back. Something stubborn and intractable, so she could walk away thinking, *See, I knew it. He's just another lucky-so-far chump who thinks he's in charge of his fate. Boy, is he in for a shock someday.*

Derek's granite features changed not one whit as he tipped his head. "Thank you for coming tonight, Ms. Holmes. It's dark out. Do you need a ride to your house, or are you alright?"

Willa's emotions slammed to a roadrunner-like halt. He was the sheriff again, *just* the sheriff. A lump filled her throat, making it hard to swallow. "I'm fine."

"Good night." With another professionally polite nod, he turned. Willa watched him walk to the end of the alley and round the corner without a backward glance.

Usually, Willa awoke a good half hour before her alarm. Taking a shower before bed, all she had to do prior to heading to work was brush her teeth, comb her hair, pull on jeans, a Something Sweet T-shirt and her work clogs and head out the door. Once again, she'd barely slept at all, however, after the scene with Derek, and on this dark winter morning, she drank black tea and watched the digital clock until it read 2:45 a.m.

Instantly speed-dialing Daisy Dunnigan, Willa waited for the grumpy, caffeine-deprived "I can't believe it's morning already" that was her best friend's characteristic greeting. A renowned New York chef, Daisy owned and operated two unpretentious but fabulous restaurants—Goodness in Soho and More Goodness in Jackson Heights—and was one of the judges on a top-rated cable cooking show. Basically, she was a star, but Willa had known her since they'd attended culinary arts school together, and they were, above all, each other's support system.

This morning, Daisy answered on the fourth ring. "Damn, what time is it?" She sounded sleepier than usual.

"Five forty-five in your neck of the woods," Willa informed. "Didn't your alarm go off?"

"It must have been about to." There was a rustling of sheets. "What's up, tootsie? How's life in Mayberry R.F.D.?"

A smile rose to Willa's face, and she was grateful already that she'd phoned. Padding to her kitchen, she pulled several carrot-raisin muffins out of a plastic container, drizzled them with water and popped them into the microwave so they would steam.

"I pissed off the sheriff," she said baldly, placing a challah bread she'd brought home from the bakery into a picnic basket.

"Sheriff McYummy?" Visiting Thunder Ridge for a weekend the previous spring, Daisy had noticed Derek immediately. "Is he still stalking you?"

"He doesn't stalk me."

"With his eyes, he does. I would *love* to be stalked by eyes the color of a Mississippi mud pie. So how'd you piss him off?"

Ignoring the comment about Derek's eyes (which, yes, were almost impossibly dark and chocolaty and, well, deep) Willa said as casually as she could, "We had a disagreement about how to handle a petty theft at the bakery. A child took a few bucks. Sheriff Neel wanted to do something about it, and I didn't. Should have been the end of the story, but we got into a… I don't know, I said some things I shouldn't have, I suppose. Now I feel guilty. I mean, the whole thing—it's no big deal, right? You can't please everyone." She shoved a can of cat food and a small plastic bowl into the basket. "You're so good at saying what you think and damn the torpedoes. That's how I want to be." She forced a laugh. "That's how I am *going* to be! I'm so glad you picked up the phone. I always feel better after we talk."

The silence on the other end was deafening. There weren't even sounds of coffee preparation. Finally, Daisy commented with uncommon gentleness. "You're starting to feel again."

Right in the solar plexus. That's where Daisy's comment struck. Waves of nausea and pain and anger washed through Willa. "I don't know what you mean," she half whispered, half gasped. "I've done nothing but feel for two years."

"No." Daisy's voice remained calm and low. "Honey, you felt pain and grief more than anyone should have to for longer than anyone should have to. Then you moved to that tiny Main Street, USA and buried yourself right along with—"

"Stop! Don't say it. Don't—" Tears choked her throat, blocking words. *No. She didn't want to feel this. Didn't have to.* She shoved the pain away. "I actually have to go to work."

"Wills," Daisy said, anxiety creeping into her voice, "I didn't mean—"

"No. It's fine."

"It's not fine!" Daisy grew adamant. "You should do more than argue with that sheriff. You need to live again. Really live."

Willa bit her bottom lip so hard, it hurt. She couldn't even remember what lust felt like.

"This was a piss-poor way to start your day, huh?"

Willa heard the self-deprecation in her friend's awkward chuckle and felt guilty. "No, it's fine." Extracting the muffins from the microwave, she tried hard to infuse her tone with positivity. "Everything is fine. I do have to go, though. I'm sorry I had to call and run."

"Right." Daisy clipped the word. "Just do me one favor, okay?"

"What?"

"Stop saying everything is fine."

A mouthful of hot black coffee kept Derek awake. He wasn't on patrol tonight, but had rolled out of bed in the wee hours, showered, dressed in street clothes then grabbed a heavy jacket and a thermos of coffee to ward off the 3:00 a.m. chill. Now, as he sat in his truck, waiting, he felt the lack of sleep catching up to him.

He wasn't up this early to watch over the streets of his town; he was up this early to watch over…

Someone.

She was late. Usually, she hit the corner of Pine and Fourth before his watch read three-oh-five. It was already ten minutes past.

"You're an idiot." Sinking down into his coat, watching the windows on the cab of his truck fog up from the cold and his breath, he thought about the previous night. Frustration welled inside him all over again.

She thought he was a joke. Out of touch. Annoying.

Insensitive toward young children. A nineteen fifties TV sitcom.

The cynicism in her voice and face last night had surprised him.

"But then, you don't really know her." That was the problem, wasn't it? He'd turned Willa into a fantasy, not a real woman. He only *thought* he knew everything he needed to. Izzy was right.

His current fatigue and irritability aside, his body reacted like a sheriff's the moment she came into view, one lone figure bundled into a puffy jacket that just barely covered her perfect jeans-clad bottom, a wool hat covering the red-gold hair that had made her blend into fall like a fairy. She typically wore her clogs on these morning strolls through town, and he was always afraid she was going to slip on black ice in those damn shoes.

Staying in the truck for the first leg of her journey, he watched as she climbed the porch steps to Belleruth Hudson's house. Belleruth was in her sixties, had famously suffered from insomnia since the death of her husband some ten years earlier and clicked her lights on around 2:00 a.m. She was one of the first customers at The Pickle Jar every morning. Willa had gotten to know her there. Shortly after Something Sweet had opened, Willa had begun carrying her picnic basket to the Hudson home in the wee hours. Sometimes she went in for a brief visit, but most of the time, like this morning, she dropped off some food and continued on her walk, in the opposite direction of Derek's truck.

He'd worn sneakers this morning, for their footstep-muffling effect. When Willa was far enough along the street that he could see her without risking her hearing him, he exited his vehicle.

There were no sidewalks in this part of town, so he

stayed close to the lawns belonging to the cottages and wood-sided, two-story homes that looped like pearls on a necklace through Thunder Ridge's downtown residential neighborhood. At the corner, Willa turned left and headed to Doc Howard Park. Derek paused, mostly hidden from view behind Rand Moser's fifth wheel. He knew it would take a few moments for Willa to complete this part of her nightly ritual, so he blew into his cold hands and waited.

Before too long, the visitor she was waiting for arrived, pausing some distance from the bench. Reaching into the basket, she withdrew the container of cat food, emptied it into a bowl and it on the ground. The cat that had slithered out of its hiding places lunged for the food and ate voraciously. When the meal was over, Willa held out her hand, presumably holding another morsel, until it dared to approach. It was the same every morning. Still as a statue, she waited for the cat to sniff her hand. Eventually it ate the tendered treat then sat and stared at her as she slipped off the bench, crouched on the frosty grass and spoke patiently until the animal allowed her to stroke it. Sometimes she tucked the skinny feline into her jacket to warm it up, but tonight a dog barked in the distance, and the cat ran off. Willa looked after it for a while then rose to collect the empty bowl.

And this was the cynical woman who had accused him of trying to recreate Mayberry.

As she continued on her walk to the bakery, Derek started after her, but slipped on a patch of black ice. Grabbing for the bike rack on the back of Rand's fifth wheel, he hung on while his feet flailed. The fifth wheel rocked, and a shouted cry of "Earthquake!" came from inside just moments before the trailer's side door banged open to more shouting. "It's The Big One!"

"Shh! For Pete's sake, be quiet, Rand!

"Who's there? Who's that?"

"It's me, Derek." Regaining his footing, Derek faced the man who had emerged wearing nothing but a pair of thermal underwear.

"Derek? Did you feel the earthquake?" Rand's question was practically a shout.

"Shhh. There was no earthquake."

Lights clicked on next door at the Newman's and across the street at Jim and Ellen Lathrop's place. *Aw, criminy.* "Rand, go back inside."

"Can't. Patty says she can hear my snoring clear into the living room."

"Well, go back in the trailer then."

"Sheriff?" Denise Newman, wrapped in a thick robe, called from her front door, "What's wrong?"

"Nothing. Please, go back in—"

"Did you feel the shaking, Denise?" Rand called to his neighbor. "This could be The Big One. I say we all gather in the center of the street."

"No! No one gather in the center of the street." Derek held up his hands. Glancing quickly toward the park, he noted it was empty. *Damn.* Willa had moved on and would now be walking by herself in the wee hours of the morning with no one to watch over her. Later this morning, he was going to talk to Izzy about changing Willa's hours, so she didn't have to go to work in the dark.

Joining the modest throng around the fifth wheel, the Lathrops arrived, huddling in their pj's. "We're all wide awake now," Jim observed in his eminently reasonable, retired radio announcer's voice. "Perhaps this would be a good time to discuss the value of forming a disaster preparedness committee in Thunder Ridge."

As murmurs of assent rose around him, Derek clapped a palm to his forehead. Patty Moser opened her front door, first asking what all the commotion was about and then offering to start a pot of coffee and make cinnamon rolls from a can. "You'll join us, won't you, Willa?"

Willa? Glancing all around until he saw a small figure standing quietly by the trailer's bumper, Derek felt his heart lurch. She was staring at him.

"I'm on my way to work, actually."

"Oh, that makes sense." Denise Newman nodded. "I didn't think you lived around here."

"Nope," Willa agreed. "I live a few blocks south." She continued to gaze at Derek. "How about you, sheriff? Do *you* live around here?" She tilted her head, brows arched. "You don't look like you're on duty."

All attention focused on him. Derek's blood pressure spiked. "I'm not on duty, no."

"What were you doing around my fifth wheel?" asked Rand. "Were you staking out someone suspicious?" He glanced around.

"No, Rand. Everything's fine. I was…doing a foot patrol."

"Off duty?" Jim asked.

Denise clasped her hands beneath her chin. "This is just why I moved from Portland. The caring, the concern. Sheriff, I sleep better knowing you're near."

"We *all* do," Patty enthused.

In the glare of the sensor light above the Mosers' garage, it was easy to see the amused quirk of Willa's lips.

"Thank you," Derek replied, "it's nice to be appreciated."

"Come inside for a cinnamon roll," Patty urged. "It'll only take a minute in the toaster oven."

"You all go ahead and go inside now, folks," Derek nodded toward the house. "I'll walk Ms. Holmes to the bakery. It's too dark to be out alone." He took Willa's arm as the party moved indoors.

Derek escorted her up the block. Once they'd cleared a couple of houses, she asked curiously, "Have you been spying on me, Sheriff?"

"Spying?"

"Yeah. It's the word we non–law enforcement folks use for sneaking around, watching people without their knowledge." Stopping, she turned toward him in the dark, barely reaching his chin. "Why have you been doing it?"

Chapter Five

"I haven't been spying on you, Willa. Spying implies looking for information. That's not what I was doing."

Without touching her again, Derek crossed the street toward the park, listening for the sound of her rubber-soled clogs following him. He stopped when he reached the bench where she sat so patiently every morning.

Patience was not the feeling that exuded from her now. Below the rim of her knitted hat, her auburn brows—so silky and perfect they looked like a child's—drew together in a troubled pucker.

Desire punched him in the gut. And upside the head. His whole life he'd waited for the feeling he got when he looked at Willa, was near Willa, thought about Willa. It was a feeling of hope so broad and deep that it set his imagination on fire. He saw them together, bodies tangled, hearts beating in time. He pictured living in a home instead of a house, lifting a laughing child who looked like her over his head. He could imagine for the first time quenching his soul-deep thirst.

And now he understood, finally, that it was just a mirage.

"You feed stray cats," he said, his voice hoarse.

She looked at him, perplexed. "So?"

"You deliver food to lonely insomniacs."

Willa blinked owlishly. "How long have you been following me?"

"Since the week the bakery opened. I was on patrol the first time I saw you walking through town. I know you work early, but two-thirty, three in the morning? No one should be out wandering the streets. I don't care how safe or quaint or backward you think this town is."

"I lived in Los Angeles, Sheriff. I've taken self-defense classes, and I carry pepper spray. I can take care of myself."

He nodded. "Glad to hear it. But Thunder Ridge is mine to protect." May as well get that out of the way. She could liken him to a TV character if she wanted, but that wasn't going to change who he was. "Mine to watch over."

"So you followed me that morning. And you've been following me ever since?"

He nodded.

"Even when you're not on duty?"

Hands in his pockets, he stared over her head. How much should he say? Did it matter? He wasn't trying to "win" her anymore. "I like a puzzle." Lowering his gaze to her face, he added, "Here's one I've been trying to solve. A beautiful woman, generous and kind, wants to be left alone, but reaches out to widows and spends hours coaxing scrawny feral cats to come to her so she can feed them. She doesn't ask anything from anyone. In fact, when you reach out to her, she takes flight like a wild bird."

Under the dim street lamp, he caught her wince. "You're trying to analyze me."

Nodding, Derek just barely refrained from touching the soft auburn waves that flowed from beneath the wool cap to caress her shoulders. "True. And, really, I should be analyzing myself. Why can't I stop thinking about you?"

The space between them buzzed and crackled like water on a hot skillet. She could have walked away then, but didn't. Derek knew that after tonight he would discipline his mind to think of anything but the woman in front of him. He would force himself to accept that she would never be his, but in these final moments of longing, he wanted one—just one—taste of the heaven he'd hoped for.

Suddenly, there was less space between them. One hand left his jacket pocket and touched the back of her head, the knitted hat rough and nubby, the auburn hair soft as a dove.

Remember it all, he told himself, knowing he wouldn't fall this hard again for a long, long time.

Willa's lips parted, and her breath escaped in a wintery puff. He could see her white, even teeth and wished not for the first time that he'd been able to make her smile or laugh more often.

"Who have you loved?"

He realized he spoke the question out loud when her eyes, misty gray and achingly beautiful, filled with tears.

"Don't," he whispered, not wanting to be the cause of her pain, remembered or otherwise. Raising his free hand, he thumbed away the first tear that fell, and a force as powerful as gravity gripped him. It was the pull of the moon, heaven reaching down to earth.

Just this once…

Her mouth was warm and sweet beneath his. He meant to stop at just the barest touch of lips, but desire fired his veins when she leaned into him. One hand cupped her jaw, the other the back of her head. He let his kiss communicate what he hadn't been able to say up to now.

He kissed the corner of her mouth, inhaled her scent, nuzzled her jaw. She let him. Her skin was like silk.

"Sorry, I didn't shave," he murmured. Sometimes before he arose to watch over her solitary walk through town, he would shave to be ready for the day ahead. He'd tossed and turned so much last night, however, that this morning he hadn't had time. "Too rough?"

In lieu of answering, she sought his lips again, and his body felt as if it were expanding to fill all of Thunder Ridge. Light as a butterfly, her hands settled atop his chest as she kissed him. He could tell when she began to surrender to the heat and the need, but then he realized something: while he was finding himself in their kiss, Willa, he sensed, was trying to lose herself, to lose for a moment the pain she refused to discuss.

Disappointment began to dull some of his lust. With one gentle, final kiss, he drew back. She seemed dazed. They stood still, foggy breath mingling in the cold, as he waited for her to steady herself.

"Almost time for you to get to work," he said roughly, as if that were an explanation for ending one of the best sensations he'd ever had. Willa was obviously perplexed.

Toward the latter part of his turbulent teens, Derek had learned the art of disciplining himself to think first, react later, but when Willa's brow knit more deeply, it was all he could do not to kiss the confusion away.

Knowing better than to keep touching her, he shoved his hands back into his jacket pockets. "Come on," he said, shooting for a lightness he sure didn't feel, "I'll stalk you to the bakery. One last shadow for old time's sake."

The irony didn't relax her. Nodding mechanically, she fell into step by his side. Neither spoke as they walked through the quiet streets of Thunder Ridge. Frustration rocked Derek's body, and his mind spun. He wondered if Willa felt the same.

Barreling through the door that was stenciled *This Way to The Pickle Jar,* Willa's boss began talking before she was fully across the threshold. "Okay, the cinnamon–hot chocolate cake was a total hit. We sold every piece at lunch, and people are asking if they can buy whole cakes. That toasted Swiss meringue frosting?" Izzy grinned. "Genius."

Willa nodded from where she was putting stickers on bags of the *zimmel* rolls that Izzy stacked by the cash register in the deli every evening. "Oh, good. Good." Distracted, she didn't even notice Izzy coming round to the clerk side of the counter until a hand shot out, grabbing one of the still-warm rolls.

"I am ravenous lately," Izzy said. "It's always that way in winter." Tearing off a hunk of the soft bread, the energetic blonde dunked it in the coffee she'd brought with her and popped it into her mouth. "So. How would you feel about baking cakes regularly? We would hire more help, of course, to free up your time. Someone else could come in early and bake the breads and rolls—although, oh my lord, you have a way with dough—and we could hire more counter help, too. Because if you agree, I'm thinking we could actually expand the bakery to provide more special occasion cakes."

"Oh, yeah?"

Izzy nodded, making her curls bounce. "You can get a basic wedding cake out here, but if you want something truly fabulous, you need to order it from Portland and transport it yourself."

"Wedding cakes?"

"It's only a thought for now." Clearly hearing Willa's

hesitation, Izzy dialed down her enthusiasm a notch. "It just seems that you know your way around flavors and decorations. And if that part of the business should take off, you could become a kind of artistic director. Anyway, mull it over." She dunked more of the roll into her coffee. "Plus, it would mean you wouldn't have to come to work so early. You could start, you know…after sunrise."

Something about her boss's tone made Willa suspicious. "After sunrise," she repeated. "I don't think so. I'd probably start the same time as usual."

"Oh. Really?" Izzy continued to dunk the roll hypnotically, unmindful of the fact that it was becoming so saturated with liquid that a sizable piece of it was about to fall off into the coffee cup. "Hmm. I don't know. There might not be enough room back there—" she gestured to the kitchen "—for you *and* someone baking the bread. And bread and coffee cakes and Danishes would be a priority, time-wise. Actually, now that I think of it, maybe we should switch up your schedule anyway. Move Norman into the opening shift. He *loves* to get up early…although, wow, you *really* do make great dough." She caught the soaked roll on her tongue just before it fell.

"Izzy," Willa ventured, "is my coming in later *your* idea?"

Izzy's faux-innocent expression was comical. "Yeah. I just thought, you know, there's a new yoga class starting at six a.m. at the community center. You wanna go? Very relaxing, I'm sure. It's just, you know…yeah."

All day, Willa had tried to understand how Derek could have begun kissing her the way he had and then stop abruptly. She'd tried to figure out whether she was glad he'd agreed not to "stalk" her in the morning anymore. And, she'd tried to tolerate the restlessness she'd felt when he'd failed to appear for his usual bagel and coffee for the first time since the bakery's grand opening.

"Did Sheriff Neel suggest I come in later?"

"What?" Izzy exclaimed, embarking on the conversational equivalent of a dog paddle. "Derek suggest that you come in later? Nooooo! Why would he? He never talks about you. At all. I mean except to say something nice. And impersonal." Izzy's fake laugh made it clear that participating in the Thunder Ridge Community Theatre would be ill-advised. "I just thought, you know, we women need our beauty rest, and it's not good to mess with our circadian rhythms." Her shoulders flagged. "Okay, yeah, it was Derek. But only because he's a very conscientious sheriff. Not for any other reason." Setting her coffee on the counter, she covered her face with her hands. "I am so bad at this. He told me not to let you know he talked to me, so please don't say anything?"

A strange, sweet relief curled through Willa's stomach. Last night the thought of his following her, watching her, getting too close raised all her alarm bells, but after that kiss… "I won't say anything," she assured.

"Thank you." Izzy's expression relaxed. "I was serious about the wedding cakes, though. Your baking is out of this world. And when you think about all the people who rent the Summit Lodge for weddings and anniversaries and birthday bashes…ooh, I would love to get a piece of that business! We wouldn't necessarily have to stay local, either."

As Izzy began to rhapsodize about a new branch of the bakery, Willa's attention drifted to dark chocolate eyes, broad shoulders, warm skin and a kiss that made her forget everything but the lips moving on hers. She couldn't figure out why he'd *stopped* kissing her, unless the experience had disappointed him? She hadn't kissed anyone in a long time; she was certainly out of practice. And he had caught her off guard. Although, let's face it, in vulnerable deep-of-the-night moments she had relived their first kiss a time or two and wondered if it would be that good again. And it had been, as far as she was concerned. Keeping her eye on the clock all morning, she'd wanted Derek to come in to order his bagel and give her a clue about where they went from here. When he'd failed to show, her mind had refused to stop thinking about him.

"I'm getting ahead of myself, aren't I?" Suddenly contrite, Izzy interrupted her own soliloquy about the business. "Never mind. I'll do some market research, and we can talk about it another time. If it doesn't suit you—"

"No, no." *For heaven's sake, focus. You're at work.* "It's a good idea. Great."

"You really think so?"

"Absolutely," Willa confirmed. "Special occasion cakes are a big industry."

"Exactly! Look at *Cake Boss*."

"That's right. And imagine the advertising possibilities. We could wear T-shirts that say Got cake? above a three-tier, tap-dancing mocha sponge covered in vanilla buttercream." Izzy's T-shirt designs were infamous. Willa joked so infrequently these days, it felt good to tease.

Izzy, who was in fact wearing a gray hoodie sporting a dancing pickle, nodded knowingly. "Fine. You're making fun of me." Grabbing a sugar packet, she slapped it against her palm before opening it and pouring it into her coffee. "Just like Derek. He disses my Pickle Jar hoodies every chance he gets, but I sold a bunch of them over Christmas."

The mention of Derek's name made heat rush to Willa's face, and Izzy noticed. "Derek had breakfast at the deli this morning," she mentioned, picking up her coffee and another roll and taking them with her to the door adjoining the deli and bakery. Before she opened it, she looked back soberly. "I've known him since he was nineteen. He's as good as they come. I'm not sure what's happening between the two of you, but if there's no chance for a relationship, please make that clear to him. Really clear. His life hasn't always been easy, and sometimes I think he—" She grimaced. "Okay, never mind. I am such a buttinsky!" She knocked herself in the head with the *zimmel* roll. "Like I'm such a relationship expert." With a wry expression, she shook her head. "Sorry. Really. Forget I spoke."

Willa gazed at her boss, letting the words sink in. *Don't hurt my friend* was what she was saying. Ashamedly, for the first time, Willa realized Derek might not be the imperturbable Rock of Gibraltar she imagined. She'd been hurting for so long that, selfishly, she forgot how easy it was to wound someone else.

"You seem to have done quite well in the relationship department," she commented admiringly, sincerely, and a pretty pink filled Izzy's cheeks.

"It took a while, but yeah."

Reunited with the father of her son, Izzy was now part of an adoring trio. But that wasn't all that Willa meant. Prior to Nate Thayer's return to Thunder Ridge, Izzy had already turned her friends and coworkers into a family.

Chewing the inside of her cheek, Willa wondered what the people in this tightknit town thought of her unwillingness to become personally involved? Perhaps she should have remained in a big, anonymous city, after all.

"Hey, isn't that the kid Derek thought stole the donation jar? Did you hire him to clean the windows?"

Willa looked at Izzy to see her peering at the large window in the front of the shop. With a spray bottle containing a blue solution in one hand and a wad of newspaper in the other, Gilberto was staring at the gold letters that spelled *Something Sweet.*

"Yes, that's him. But I didn't hire him." Willa walked around the counter. "What's he doing?"

"Looks like he's going to wash the windows. I wonder if he's trying to earn money? Why don't you ask him, and if that's what he's trying to do, pay him out of petty cash. He can come next door, too."

Willa nodded, waiting for Izzy to close the door to the diner before she headed outside. Gilberto startled a bit when he saw her, even though he knew she worked there. Guilt crawled across his features. He and Willa knew what Izzy did not, of course: that he *had* stolen the money.

"Hello."

"Hi," he mumbled.

"What are you doing?"

"I'm gonna clean your windows."

"Well, thank you, but I actually cleaned them this morning. Are you trying to earn money?" If he was, she would send him next door right away.

He shook his head. "I can't earn money for this. I'm supposed to do it for free."

"Supposed to?"

"When you didn't tell on me, the sheriff said you saved my butt, and I better figure out how to show you I'm worth it."

"So you decided to wash the bakery windows?"

"No. The sheriff, he said I look like a good window washer. And after I wash the windows, I'm gonna sweep inside the bakery."

What? "That sounds like a very long afternoon. What grade are you in?"

"Sixth."

Sixth. That made him eleven or twelve. Remembrance

pierced Willa like an arrow. "I'm sure you have homework—"

"Sheriff's going to help me. Afterward. I come here every afternoon when school's out, and then he helps me with math and stuff. Then he's going to drive me home. He's driving me *in the squad car.*"

"Every day? Is that what the sheriff told you to do?"

"He says a boy runs away, but a man pays his debts. So I'm here, paying them."

The tug on Willa's heart was not the least bit comfortable. "I appreciate what you're doing, and the sheriff was right about making restitution for what you took, but, um..." A thought, stuck her. "Does your cousin agree to this?"

Gilberto's gaze shifted downward. "He doesn't know," he mumbled.

"Gilberto," she began carefully.

The boy's eyes widened. "The sheriff's here to check on me. I gotta get to work." Spraying the windows with vigor, Gilberto used the wadded newspaper to scrub the glass.

Willa turned around, to where Gilberto had been looking, and there, indeed, was Derek, striding down the street with his customary confidence. His features were neutral, unreadable. When he made eye contact with her, Willa couldn't see his expression change one bit, even though her body reacted instantly and without her permission, simply to the sight of him.

She was pretty sure that for the rest of her life, when she thought about Derek Neel, she would picture him first in his uniform. Its desert-sand color was a perfect complement to his deeply tan complexion and black hair. Crisp, always perfectly ironed, the uniform emphasized his lean, muscular frame, which in turn spotlighted his height. He looked like he could whip the bad guys with a flick of his wrist.

Exactly how a lawman should look.

Why had she called him a TV sitcom sheriff? That was so hurtful. So unlike her. And, really, if he did remind her of a TV sheriff, it was in all the good ways. He was honest and ethical, and he made people feel better. Safer.

"Afternoon, Ms. Holmes." He tipped his head to her, and she noticed he'd had his hair cut. The thick waves were shorter on the sides.

"Sheriff."

"Gilberto," he said. "Right on time."

"I was early."

Derek's eyes glinted with approval. "Good man."

Gilberto nodded, hair the same shade as Derek's flopping into his eyes. Standing taller, prouder, he used both hands to wipe down the window.

Willa was struck by the similarity between the two of them. They both had café au lait skin, hair as dense as a string mop, and eyes so dark it was hard to distinguish the iris from the pupil.

"Sheriff," she said, "may I speak with you, please? In the bakery?"

He glanced at his watch. "I have a couple of minutes." *Only* a couple, his tone stated.

"Fine." She led the way inside and rubbed her arms as warm, bread-scented air welcomed them in from the cold. "Would you like a cup of coffee?"

"No, thank you."

All right. Down to business. "Sheriff, I think what you're doing with Gilberto is admirable. No one could argue that you're influencing him in a positive way. But I would rather that you leave me…leave the bakery…out of it."

"Yes, you made that clear."

"Well, then you can see that his being here every day when I am trying to stay out of it might be awkward."

Derek appeared to ponder what she was saying. "Actually, no. How is it awkward? He's just a kid doing some chores."

Emotionally speaking, there was no such thing as "just a kid doing some chores." Not in Willa's world. And especially not when the kid was preteen and obviously aching for a parent.

"He could go to the deli. Izzy was saying she could use someone to do the windows over there. I have plenty of time in the mornings, so I always clean the bakery windows myself."

"Gilberto stole from the bakery. He's going to make amends to the bakery."

"Actually, he stole from the donation jar—"

"Same difference."

Derek's body and even his tone remained calm, but he was as immovable as the mountain that stood sentry over their town.

Willa swallowed, her initial fear turning into embarrassment that she was, once again, making a big deal of something in front of Derek. "Sure, sure. I don't mind taking a break from window washing for a few days."

"There was almost a hundred dollars in the jar. It'll be more than a few days. And I'd like to suggest you empty the jar more frequently."

He sounded impersonal, as if he was giving safety tips to the senior center. She said nothing.

"Was there anything else you needed to discuss?" he asked.

Yes, why did you stop kissing me last night?

"No. That was it."

"Alright." Derek glanced to the window, where Gilberto was working particularly hard on a spot. "I'll be supervising him. If anything comes up, call me."

She nodded. *Don't let him go. Find out why he didn't come to the bakery this morning. Tell him...tell him you missed seeing him.* Because it was true. There had been a gaping hole in her morning routine.

"Sheriff!" she called as he headed toward the door. Derek looked back. "I didn't thank you last night. For watching me on my way to work. I've become used to taking care of myself, so… Well, I'd just like to say thank you. I should have said it last night."

The muscles in his face relaxed. His eye color seemed to change from cold onyx to hot fudge. After gazing at her for a time without speaking, Derek gave a small shake of his head, more to himself than for her. "That's a relief," he said finally. "Now I won't have to figure out new ways to stay out of sight."

"You mean you're going to keep following me?"

"It's not safe to walk around town at three a.m." His rapid return to law enforcement mode made him look very, very cute. "If you insist on going for walks before work, I'll have to keep watch. Unless you're planning a change in schedule?"

Willa feigned an innocent expression. "You mean like if my job description were to change? If I started decorating cakes or something, for example?"

Derek rubbed his brow. "Izzy obviously handled that well."

Willa smiled. "Don't blame her. I'd probably still come to work early. I'm already awake in the morning, so—" She stopped, but not before raising his curiosity.

"Awake before three?" She expected him to question her about *why* she was awake so early, but instead he commented, "It's supposed to be a creative time, the very early morning. In days gone by, more people were awake in the wee hours. They worked or visited with neighbors. Or made love." He nodded. "Very powerful time."

There wasn't an iota of suggestiveness in his tone, but heat rose inside Willa like mercury in a thermometer. She felt herself blush from the tip of her toes to the top of her head.

"You can Google it," he added.

"I'll do that." Her voice was hoarse.

"Good afternoon, Ms. Holmes."

"Good afternoon, Sheriff."

Chapter Six

Crossing her arms on the desk, Holliday Bailey, local librarian and continual burr under Derek's saddle, beamed up at him. "I told you, in order to fulfill your request for a library card, I will need two pieces of mail with the potential cardholder's name and address."

"And I told you, I don't have two pieces of mail with Gilberto's name and address. So, can you make an exception?"

Holliday gasped. "What? Are you, Sheriff Follows-The-Rules, asking me to make an exception in library protocol for you? To, in fact, *break the rules*?" She placed a heavily jeweled hand over her chest. "I'm shocked. I'm appalled. I'm… I'm feeling faint." She glanced around. "Medic?"

"Hilarious," Derek affirmed since she seemed to need that. "You're hilarious. Now can you give me the library card, please?"

She started to respond, then looked beyond him. "Hi,

Willa! What can I do for you?" Glancing back at Derek, she widened her eyes. *Look who's here!*

Derek gritted his teeth. Holliday was one of Izzy's best friends. As such, Holliday and Derek had spent more time together than they otherwise would have. Over the past year plus, she'd figured out he had a crush on Willa.

"Hi," Willa responded, approaching the reference desk. "Hello, Sheriff."

"Ms. Holmes."

Holliday laughed. "You're so formal, you two. Let me introduce you. Derek, meet Willa. Willa, this is Derek."

As if God wove strands of hair out of autumn leaves, Willa's soft waves cascaded around her shoulders as she smiled his way. "Sheriff," she acknowledged, steadily meeting his eyes.

"Ms. Holmes," he responded once again, and the moment became private, all theirs, as together they affirmed that they would not be pushed around.

"Hopeless." Holliday wagged her head. "I have that book you put on hold, Willa. *Decorating with Gum Paste.* Looks fascinating."

"It is. But if you're helping Sheriff Neel, I can wait."

"I'm trying to get a library card for Gilberto," Derek shared. "He's never had one."

"Never?" Instantly, Willa's brow furrowed with concern. "I would think he'd need one for school, if nothing else."

Gilberto had been working at the bakery for almost a week. Derek picked him up in the squad car or in his truck—both of which Gilberto loved—after work, and drove him out of town to the house he shared with his cousin's family. Invariably, Gilberto would mention that Willa had provided a snack. He also said that she corrected his grammar, and when he stayed late asking for more chores, she told him he should be doing his homework or playing a sport. Gilberto seemed to like that she talked to him that way.

"He does need a library card." Derek studied Willa, wondering if she would always remain a puzzle to him. She had seemed almost frantically opposed to Gilberto working at the bakery at first, yet she cared about his welfare. She'd protested when she'd found out Derek was following her, yet kissed him back. Kissed him hungrily.

"Here's the application." Holliday slid a rectangular printed card toward Derek. "Fill it out to the best of your ability. Let me get your hold, Willa." Pushing away from the desk, she rose and walked away on teetering high heels.

There were few similarities between Willa and the librarian. Holliday's bold, in-your-face sex appeal was a lightning storm; Willa's soft sensuality reminded him of a gentle rain. Not that she was simple, though. Nope. Anything but.

"So." Off duty, Derek slipped a hand in the pocket of his jeans. "Anything new?"

"Yes, actually. I'm thinking about decorating wedding cakes." She grinned. After unzipping the puffy white jacket that made her look like she was about to push off a ski slope, Willa unwound the raspberry-colored scarf around her neck. "Gilberto told me you're helping him with homework. Sounds as if he's behind in most of his classes?"

"All of them. A couple of years behind in math. I spoke with his teacher. He has no learning disabilities, just a poor attendance record since first grade."

"What happened in first grade?"

Derek glanced around the area in which they stood. Gilberto lived outside of town, but he attended school in

Thunder Ridge. He had a right to some privacy. "Are you really interested in this?" he asked.

Willa looked offended at first then seemed to understand why he would ask. "Yes," she said solemnly. "I'm interested."

"I'm off duty. If you have a couple of minutes, I can fill you in once we're done here."

Willa nodded. Derek filled out the application for the library card with as much information as he knew. When Holliday returned with Willa's book, he handed her the application. In return, she gave him a plastic library card on which she instructed him to write Gilberto's name.

"I can take that to the front desk." Holliday pointed to the cake-decorating book in Willa's hand.

"Don't bother. We'll use your self-checkout," he said.

"Want me to walk you through?" Holliday asked him with feigned concern, her implication obviously that he was going to have trouble.

"Between the two of us, I think we'll manage."

"Yes, two is always better than one." She smiled benignly, but Derek knew she'd be on the phone to Izzy before he and Willa were out the door.

"Holliday was behaving a bit oddly," Willa commented as they emerged from the library.

"Holliday *is* a bit odd," Derek groused, but in truth the flaming redhead was more outrageous than odd. With her leopard-print sweaters and platform shoes, she was no one's idea of a small-town librarian. "She likes to poke at me."

"Hmm."

It was another cold winter day. Willa was already zipping her coat again.

"Let's find someplace warm and private, and I'll tell you what I know about Gilberto," he said.

"Someplace private doesn't exist in Thunder Ridge." Willa smiled as she wrapped herself in the scarf.

Derek's fingers itched with the urge to free her hair from beneath the knitted tube. "Do you have anywhere you need to be?"

"No. It's my day off."

"I know. I slept in."

Willa's pretty lips pursed as her smile widened. "You're doing a good job."

"At what?"

"Hiding when you follow me. I haven't seen you once all week."

Which meant she'd looked. "I've had practice."

Lately, it was all he could do at three in the morning not to join her on the park bench when she was feeding the damn cats and make out with her under the stars. But what had changed? He didn't want a relationship that was a mosaic of secrets.

"Come on." Escorting her to his restored fifty-seven pickup, he couldn't squelch the flash of pride and pleasure when she ran her fingers over the highly polished red hood.

"This is beautiful. How long have you had it?"

"Since I was nineteen. It'll be warm if I turn on the heat, and it's private if you don't mind sitting in a truck in the parking lot."

"I don't mind at all."

Opening the door, Derek had a feeling of déjà vu as she climbed in. How many times had he imagined Willa snuggling against him in the cab?

"Is it authentically restored?" she asked, touching the dashboard as he slid in on the driver's side.

"When I was nineteen, my friend Walt offered me a chance to restore the truck with him. I thought we were restoring it for him, and that was okay with me. It was the most fun I'd ever had. We worked on it for two years whenever he had spare time. In the second year, he let me work on it alone."

"He must have been a very good friend."

"The best."

Derek put the key in the ignition and let the engine idle so the heater could work. "Should get warm in here in a minute." Relaxing against the embossed vinyl seat back, he rested his wrist on a steering wheel that was approximately the diameter of an extra-large pizza. "Walt was a great man."

"How did you meet him?"

"Walt Martin was the sheriff of Thunder Ridge for nearly three decades. We met shortly after I arrived in Oregon. I'd been living with an uncle and aunt I didn't get along with very well, and I headed out on my own at seventeen. Back then my favorite sport was fighting anyone who was willing." Willa's slack-jawed surprise was almost comical.

"I'd been bumming around Portland," he continued. "I made my way out here, because I wanted someplace new to steal from." This time, he almost laughed out loud at Willa's expression. "I like to think I've changed for the better."

"So what kind of shenanigans brought you and Walt together?"

"I was a really clumsy burglar. Tripped alarms, alerted dogs. I never actually made it all the way into anyone's house, but I scared quite a few people. As the sheriff, Walt decided that rather than arresting me, he would take me under his wing. He held me accountable, though. I had to apologize to everyone I'd attempted to burgle. Walt saved my life."

Willa's once-again kind, always gorgeous, silver-blue

eyes glittered with understanding. "You're paying it forward with Gilberto."

He didn't need her admiration to know he was doing the right thing, but it sure felt good.

"Did Walt give you the truck when you were done working on it?" Willa asked.

"In a way. He offered to let me buy it, but for much less than he could have gotten from anyone else. He knew it would mean more to me if I could sit in it and say, 'I earned this.' Of course, at the time I had no idea he was deep, deep discounting it for me. All I knew was that it was the first thing I'd ever owned, and it made me feel like a king. In later years, I tried to pay him more, but he always refused to take my money. He said I could pay for the truck by being the man he knew I could be."

"So you became a sheriff like him."

"I'll be lucky to be half the man Walt Martin was. But, yes, I wanted to be a sheriff, because I saw how much he gave to the community. How much he belonged to it and how the community belonged to him."

The glance she gave him was heart-meltingly sincere, and suddenly the cold winter day felt like summer in the cab of his truck. Without a few dozen more sets of fingers and toes, it would be difficult to count the number of times he'd imagined being with Willa as they drove the River Loop on a day off from work, or parked behind the hay bales for the summer drive-up movies at Gold Meadow Farm. Sitting in a parking lot together was nowhere near the same as the scenarios he'd played out in his mind, but if this was as close as he was ever going to get, well, he'd take it.

He'd make a mental snapshot of her, this haunting, elusive woman whom he'd sometimes thought about day and night, and he'd store the memory away, taking it out when he needed a buffer against the solitary times ahead.

Willa couldn't believe she had dissed this very good man. "I truly am sorry I made that comment about TV sheriffs," she began.

He stopped her with a laugh. "I'm a big Andy Griffith fan. I like Westerns, too." His expression—amused, self-deprecating, and irresistibly boyish—made her toes curl in her boots.

"You know, I think Gilberto is a lot like me. He needs to belong somewhere. I never felt like part of something until Walt showed me I could be part of Thunder Ridge. It made all the difference to my motives. Changed me in a way I might otherwise have missed." He fiddled with the heat knob. "You warm enough?"

Willa nodded. It was impossible to feel cold sitting so close to him.

"Gilberto's parents are out of the picture," Derek went on, turning the subject toward the boy who was the reason they'd climbed into the truck to begin with.

A stab of frustration surprised her. She wanted to hear more about Derek. Marshaling her focus, she nodded for him to continue.

"According to his school records, he was being raised by an aunt who was a single parent with a few kids of her own. When the burden on her became overwhelming, Gilberto moved in with one cousin or another until he wound up with Roddy. Gilberto's teachers say he's smart and is always eager to learn when the school year begins, but as the lessons pick up steam, he falls behind and his absences begin to increase. It's a vicious cycle. Since first grade, he's been truant nearly fifty percent of the time."

Willa gasped.

"At this point," Derek said, "it's a pattern everyone's come to accept. But we're going to break the pattern."

So determined. So confident.

"Can the school give him extra support?" she asked.

"He doesn't qualify. Truancy isn't a learning disorder." Derek's fingers drummed the steering wheel. "Academics weren't my strength, but I'm going to help him any way I can."

Eyes narrowed, jaw set, he looked like a cross between heroic warrior and plain old determined dad when he spoke like that.

Gazing thoughtfully out the windshield, Willa made eye contact with Jeanne Frank and Myra Newsome as the duo crossed the parking lot on their way to the library. Both women exhibited obvious surprise at seeing her in the truck with Derek. Jeanne waved wildly, and Willa raised her hand limply in response. Myra was an inveterate gossip. Tempted to sink low in her seat, Willa looked at Derek for his response. If he noticed the women at all, he didn't seem to care that he and Willa were about to become headline news. He was still watching her.

"I thought you should know more about Gilberto," he was saying. "I want you to understand the impact that doing chores at the bakery is going to have on his life. I know, or I think I know, that it's been hard for you to have him there."

"Not hard," she said carefully. "He's fun to be around. He hums and dances now when he works."

Surprise and then gratification deepened Derek's smile.

"You'd be a good father," Willa blurted before she had time to think. She reached toward the dash, trailing her fingertips along the smooth, shiny red metal. It was cold, of course, a hundred and eighty degrees different from his skin, which had been warm the other night and downright hot to the touch the evening they'd made out after leaving the White Lightning Tavern together.

"I make whole grain bagels now," she said overly loudly to fill the conversational vacuum left by her awkwardness. "They're good, not too heavy." Her eyes were still trained on the dashboard rather than on the man who kept it polished. "We have a new cream cheese, too. Sweet Marionberry. In case you were thinking about coming in for breakfast again. Sometime."

Dear lord. Bagels and cream cheese? Seriously? Why couldn't she simply say what was on her mind? "We make our own jam now." *Oh, please.* "You haven't been in for a while, is the thing, and…you're missed. By everyone. All the regulars, everyone who's there in the morning, you know, misses seeing you." *Coward.*

Derek's expression did not say, "*This chick is crazy*," but she figured that's what he was thinking. She needed to get honest. Just spit out what she wanted. And what she wanted was…?

His touch. His warmth to melt the chill in her soul. She wanted the feeling his arms and his lips had given her—the feeling of summer in the midst of an achingly long personal winter.

Her throat threatened to close with nerves, but she forced herself to speak. "I've missed seeing you, too."

One second passed. Then two. As she counted to five, she began to worry, stopped fiddling with the dashboard and chanced a look at his face.

Derek's brows were still pulled together. Rather than softening, his features were once again set in stern granite. "I need to head to the office. I have some paperwork to do."

Whoa. For the first time since she was engaged to be married, she'd told a man she liked him and that was his response? *"I need to head to the office"?* Attempt to flirt with the sheriff: total fail.

"Do you need a ride somewhere?" he asked, clearly being polite. "I can drop you at—"

"No. No, no," she said cheerily, her hand already going to the door. "Such a beautiful day. I'm going to walk. That's what I was doing before I stopped at the library, actually. I was walking. I do that now later in the day. In fact—" extricating herself from this embarrassing situation now seemed tantamount to anything else "—I'm not going to walk in the morning at all anymore. Nope. I'll just drive myself to work. Sleep in a bit. Walk when other people are out walking. So, you won't have to follow me around." She emitted a trill of laughter that sounded faintly maniacal. "You'll be able to sleep in, too. Unless you're working, of course, following suspicious people. But you won't have to follow *me*." Now he was scowling and looking at her as if he might call for backup. She opened the door and slid out. "Bye."

She gave a quick wave, shut the door and was off, walking as quickly as she could toward home.

That could have gone worse, she thought, nodding to herself. If there had been, say, a sudden tornado-like gust of wind that picked up the truck with them in it, whirled it through the air and dropped them on top of the General Store, sending terrified shoppers running for their lives into the street, that would have been worse.

Willa watched her square-toed boots eat the pavement. He'd kissed her, she'd kissed him back, he'd changed his mind. End of story. Not flattering, not encouraging, but certainly not the end of the world. And maybe she was being protected. Maybe she only *thought* she was ready for a man's arms, for his company, for the physical plunge that offered oblivion even as it reminded a person she was, in fact, very much alive.

"I need a hobby," she muttered.

As time marched on, Willa decided, she would try very hard to be proud of herself for acknowledging that she wanted the sheriff to kiss her again. For the first time in nearly two years, she had been willing to admit she needed something more than a life frozen in time and memory. For just a moment, she'd glimpsed the spring thaw, and she'd been glad.

Chapter Seven

She handled the DVD delicately, reverently, the way one might handle a Fabergé egg, removing it from its case, blowing specs of dust off its glassy surface, touching it only by the edges as she set it in the DVD player and closed the little door. The motor whirred, the TV screen assured her that her video was loading and gave her enough time to seat herself on the edge of her couch, her posture and her breathing both strained.

This was something Willa hadn't watched in the past two years, unlike the other home videos she had watched and rewatched so many times that she'd finally burned them onto additional discs to avoid losing them.

When the menu screen came up, she chose Play All. A young woman dressed in bridal lace and satin appeared on the screen, grinning at the camera as a small group of bridesmaids surrounded her. They were helping her don a garter, and the bride, with cascading auburn hair held back on one side by a jeweled clip, looked up at the camera and mugged, waggling her brows and pursing her lips in mock flirtation.

The next scene showed Willa again, this time walking toward her groom, who grinned like a fool. Lighthearted, winsome joy defined the ceremony and reception, befitting two kids who were barely out of their teens, but sure they had found their forever.

As the wedding portion of the video wrapped up, the screen went dark then lit again with a beatifically smiling Willa, only a year older, and a sleeping baby wrapped in the palest pink. The tiny girl had cupid's bow lips, skin like strawberries and cream, and auburn lashes that fanned her round cheeks as she snoozed. Willa cuddled her daughter close and looked at the camera, mouthing so as not to wake the baby, *I love us*.

The video stopped then started again. This time Willa was behind the camera, and her husband, Jason, held their still-sleeping Sydney. Jason's face, trustworthy and triangle-jawed, open and approachable (perfect for the doctor he planned to become, everyone always said) beamed contentment. Unlike Willa, he had no fear of waking Syd, because he complained that she was never awake enough when he was home.

Now he looked straight into the camera lens and proclaimed, "I'm the luckiest man in the world." The pride and gratitude in his eyes left no doubt that he was sincere.

Picking up the remote, Willa hit Stop. She remembered that day so well, zooming into Jason's face so that in the decades to come their daughter would see her father's eyes and know: *you are loved fully and completely.*

Tossing the remote onto the coffee table as if it were burning her fingers, she rose and wrapped her arms around herself. She had loved that life. Had felt grateful for every single day, even the messy ones, the boring ones, the worrisome ones. Never in a million years had she thought it would end so soon.

Still hugging herself tightly, Willa crossed to the window and looked out. After the sunny morning, the afternoon sky had turned gray. Now Thunder Ridge was being sprinkled with a dusting of snow. School was out for the day, and the kids across the street were standing on their lawn, jacketed arms outstretched, heads back and mouths open as they caught snowflakes on their tongues.

Their joy was vivid and fresh and real. Hers was a faded photograph, something she could no longer feel, only take out and look at. She felt as if she were fading, too.

"This is no good." Moving quickly, she grabbed her jacket off a hall tree, jammed her arms in, slipped on her boots and went outside. At first she didn't know where she was headed, but as she marched along, snatches of her conversation with Derek played in her mind, and she followed their path.

According to the sheriff, Gilberto needed focused help to catch up to his academic benchmarks. If he didn't catch up, his future would be dim, for sure, yet the school couldn't provide the extra help the boy needed. Derek didn't think he was capable, and tutors were expensive. Willa, on the other hand, was familiar with fifth-grade curriculum.

An idea began to take shape in her mind.

Checking her watch, she saw that it wasn't yet four o'clock. Gilberto's teacher might still be at school. Her footsteps struck the sidewalk with more resolve.

The snow was delicate, melting as it touched the ground, and merely being out in it made her feel more alive. By the time she reached Vista Road, leading to the elementary school, Willa knew exactly what she wanted to do.

* * *

"I'm telling you, dude, it's her birthday, and she's not doing nothing."

"Anything."

Gilberto growled. "That's what she always does. Tells me how to talk. Anything…nothin'…whatever. That's not the point."

"It's absolutely the point." Derek turned from the window, where he'd been contemplating his thoughts more than the view outside his office. "Your education is the reason Willa started tutoring you. She wants you to have a future."

"Yeah, which is why I want her to have a present for her birthday. You get it, dude? She cares about my *future*, I want her to have a *present*. Oh, man, I'm good."

"Uh huh. You are good." Since the evening Gilberto sped off with the donation jar, he'd changed from a furtive kid who seemed moody and awkward around adults, to an outgoing, far more confident young man. And the change in the two weeks since Willa had begun to tutor him in all his subjects was even more profound. Derek wasn't sure what had sparked the change in Willa, but her willingness to help Gilberto had unlocked a door.

Gilberto might still voice a casual attitude toward his schoolwork, but now that he was beginning to grasp a few things, his posture was straighter. He looked happier, chatted more and was currently chatting with Derek about Willa's birthday, which was, apparently, tomorrow.

"Izzy, she come into the bakery—"

"Came into the bakery."

"I *know*. Dude!" The boy took a noisy deep breath. "Okay…*came* into the bakery, 'cause she needed Willa to fill something out, and she said—I totally heard her—'Hey, girl, your birthday is tomorrow.'"

"I've never heard Izzy say 'Hey, girl.'"

Gilberto shrugged. "I mighta got that wrong, but then Willa said, 'Yeah, I've got plans after work,' but, Dude, she don't. Wait—I know, *doesn't.*"

"How do you know she doesn't?"

"Because I asked her if she could help me with my homework tomorrow, and she said, 'Sure.'"

"Her plans are probably for evening, Gilberto." Derek told himself not to wonder what those plans were, or with whom she was sharing them.

Two weeks ago, Willa told him she wanted him to come back to the bakery, and he'd had to force himself not to think about her, not to convince himself it was okay just to drop in to get a bagel and coffee or to see how Gilberto was doing. True, that day in his truck she had seemed to be telling him she was interested, after all. But he knew too much now. He knew Willa was not ready for all the things he wanted. And, he knew he wasn't ready to settle for less.

"She doesn't have *any* plans. That's what I'm trying to *tell* you." Impatience colored the boy's voice. "I told her I got a test on Friday, so could she help me a little longer tomorrow, and she said, 'Yeah, I've got plenty of time.' See? She forgot what she told Izzy."

"Or maybe she's making you her first priority." To give himself something to do, Derek reached for a stack of papers on his desk. "Want to hand me that stapler?" he asked the boy who was sitting in his desk chair, swiveling left and right in agitation.

Gilberto grabbed the heavy black stapler and handed it over the desk. "I'm telling you, she's not doing noth—*anything* for her birthday. And that's not cool, 'cause she's, you know, she's nice. She's good to people."

Derek nodded. Shortly after their conversation in his truck, Willa had told Gilberto that she was going to help him with school, and she was, apparently, quite proficient at it. “Like a real teacher, except that I understand her,” Gilberto had become fond of saying.

Gilberto was a good person, too. He came to the office after finishing his jobs and his homework at the bakery. Derek had spent time with Gilberto the past two weekends, too. They had gone ice-skating at the temporary rink Jax Stewart set up in Trillium Park. Then they went to the movies, where Gilberto ate popcorn and chocolate-covered caramels until Derek was sure he was going to be sick. Derek’s days off were more full and more fun than they had been since Nate Thayer had come to town, claiming Derek’s best friend as his bride.

And now his new little buddy wanted to do something for Willa’s birthday. Self-preservation warned Derek to change the subject. Pronto. But the image of Willa celebrating her birthday alone overruled. He squinted at Gilberto. “What do you have in mind?”

Willa did her marketing on Friday evenings. The large grocery store outside of town stayed fairly quiet at night, and she was able to wander the aisles, looking at ingredients and wondering what she could experiment with for the bakery. She saw no reason to alter her pattern on this particular Friday.

She’d already had phone calls from her parents, her aunt Esther and cousin Nancy. Daisy had phoned, too, singing “Happy I-Can’t-Believe-We’re-This-Old-Day to You” on Willa’s voice mail then asking, “What are you doing tonight? It had better be good, and it had better involve a man.”

Thirty-four is not old, Willa had texted back. Big plans for the evening. Many men involved. XOXO.

At the market, she had a nice conversation with the

butcher, who, yes, was a man. Then she chatted with the cashier, also male, and declined help out from the bagger, another XY chromosome carrier. So she hadn't lied, exactly.

Putting her groceries in the trunk of her car, she got in, turned the key in the ignition and hoped the heater would work quickly. After spending the afternoon helping Gilberto study for a math test he had the following week, she was surprisingly hungry. She planned to make a toasted pancetta and brie cheese sandwich with a smear of the homemade fig jam they sold at the bakery. Then she would eat in front of the television, watching an episode of *Downton Abbey* on Netflix. There was nothing wrong with spending her birthday like that, even if her family and Daisy disagreed.

Pointing her car toward home, she traveled less than a quarter mile before she saw a trio of lights flashing in her rearview mirror. Though no siren wail accompanied the lights, Willa knew she was looking at the lights of a police car. She pulled over, wondering what she had done wrong.

Rolling down her window, she smiled, hoping she could talk her way out of a huge fine on her birthday, "Hello, what did I do— Oh. Hi."

Derek nodded, looking official in his uniform and even a hat, which she rarely saw him wear. "Evening. Are you aware your undercarriage is sparking?"

"My...what is what?"

"I saw sparks coming from the undercarriage of your car. That's very dangerous. I've alerted the local fire department, who I'm sure will arrive shortly. For now, I'm going to have to ask you to step out of the vehicle for safety's sake." He spoke quickly, which emphasized the danger of the situation. "If you'd like to bring your purse and any other belongings you need to take with you, I'll have Dan Bowman tow the car in and look at it." He attempted to open her door, which was locked. "Dan will contact you. Will you unlock your door, please?"

Confused as heck and growing more alarmed, Willa clicked the lock. Immediately, Derek opened the door and reached for her arm to help her out. "Let's move quickly," he said.

"We're not even in Thunder Ridge," Willa grumbled. "What are you doing out here?"

"I'm a county employee. You're in my county. Now, do you need anything besides your purse?"

"I just went to the grocery store."

"Okay, get in the squad car, please. I'll grab the groceries."

She did as he asked, realizing as she slid onto the front seat of the police car that she was asking him to risk his safety for her pancetta. She watched him, big and strong and sure, and was going to call out to him to forget the groceries when he returned, three bags in his hands. He stowed everything in the backseat then slid into the driver's spot. The car filled with his presence. She felt sure she could smell his pheromones.

With supreme effort, she returned her attention to the car. "Where are the sparks?" she asked.

"They were visible while you were driving. It's a good sign that it stopped when you cut the engine. So." He glanced her way. "Got any plans for the weekend?"

"Is it okay to leave the car there if it could catch on fire?" She craned her neck to look back.

"Like I said, it stopped sparking. And I'm sure a fire truck will be there soon. Weekend plans?" he asked again.

The night was starting to feel truly surreal. Derek hadn't spoken to her this much in weeks. These days, she saw him mostly in passing or through the window of the bakery if he dropped by to pick up Gilberto. He didn't come in. She'd come to accept that whatever attraction he'd felt for her had ended, and she tried not to think about why.

"I'm working on Sunday," she said. "I thought I'd do some cooking tomorrow. Freeze a few dinners." *Wow. That ought to make his head spin with excitement.* "Maybe I'll take a drive into Portland." The urban area was a good ninety minutes away by car. And, actually, it seemed even further removed with regard to lifestyle. The uber-popular, quirky city couldn't be more different from the charming western vibe of Thunder Ridge.

"What are you going to do in Portland?"

Uh, nothing. Because I just made it up. "I might go to Powell's." She mentioned the multistory independent bookstore that was on every visitor's must-see list. "And I love Northwest 23rd." That much, at least, was true. Northwest 23rd boasted some of the city's best shops and eateries. Maybe she really ought to drive over. Get out of her rut.

"Have you ever eaten at El Gaucho?"

Willa shook her head.

"It's downtown in the Benson Hotel. Best steaks this side of Texas."

"You've been to Texas?"

"I'm from Texas," he confirmed.

"I assumed you grew up in the Pacific Northwest."

"I did." In the lights from the dashboard, she saw him smile wryly. "I 'grew up' here. Became a man instead of a would-be felon. But I was born in Lubbock, Texas, and lived there until I was almost seventeen. That's when the uncle I was living with told me to straighten up or get out. I chose to get out. Started hitchhiking and ended up here, thank God."

He kept surprising her. "You really did have a hard childhood."

Derek shrugged. "I had challenges." They drove in silence for a good quarter mile before he spoke again. "Gilberto is confused, because the only people he feels he belongs with are the ones he can't relate to. They're people he doesn't want to become, and they're not what I'd call attentive. *Not* belonging to them, though, makes him feel panicked. Like a boat bobbing alone in the middle of the ocean. He wants mooring, and he'll take it where he can get it. Even if that means looking for it in all the wrong places."

Everything he said made sense, but somehow his words left her with a burning discomfort in the pit of her stomach. "You're offering him the chance to belong somewhere," she observed. "You're doing everything you can to help."

He cut a glance at her. "*You're* giving him the opportunity to belong, too. Every time you work with him."

"But my help is temporary." Suddenly, she felt sick with worry. "Maybe the last thing he needs is someone transient in his life. What if that makes things worse?"

"What you're giving him isn't temporary, Willa. The time you spend with Gilberto is something he'll take with him wherever he goes, from now on." He paused. "And how do you know when your relationship with him is going to end? It doesn't have an expiration date."

They were nearing Thunder Ridge. The twinkle lights that had decorated every building since the weekend after Thanksgiving were becoming visible, a sweet beacon to guide them down an otherwise dark road. Derek had stopped talking, the silence in the car unexpectedly welcome as Willa tried to make sense of her feelings.

All her life, she'd had a place and people to whom she'd belonged. Why did talking about belonging, even thinking about it, make her feel so nettled? Being hesitant to put down roots in Thunder Ridge did not mean she didn't belong...somewhere. And if it turned out that all she was doing here was helping a young preteen set down roots that would allow him to grow tall, that ought to be enough.

As they reached the downtown area, Derek turned up Warm Springs Road. After 6:00 p.m., even on a Friday night, most of the businesses were dark, though a couple of diehards, notably the General Store and the pet shop that had opened last year, remained well lit and open for business. As Derek approached Fourth Street, Willa alerted, "You can turn here for me." His cell phone rang, and he answered it, passing the street. "Or not," she murmured.

"Hey, Izz," he said, using his Bluetooth. "Oh, yeah? Well, I'm close to the deli… Sure, I can check it for you… Right-o. Bye." He looked at Willa. "Octavio thinks he forgot to turn off the burners this afternoon. Izzy's at some function with Nate and asked me to stop by and take a look. Do you mind coming along?"

"No, I don't mind. That's really weird. Octavio crosses every *T*. If anything, he's a tad obsessive."

"We all have an off day occasionally."

"I guess so."

Derek drove around the corner and into the alley behind The Pickle Jar. "Come with me," he said to Willa. "You can show me how to turn off the burners."

As they stood at the back door, she asked, "How long have you had keys to Izzy's restaurant?"

"Pretty much forever. Henry and Sam gave them to me years ago." Henry and Sam Bernstein had owned and operated the deli for decades before giving 60 percent of the business to Izzy, who'd started out as a waitress and manager before becoming their partner. The two men had happily semiretired and were currently at a cousin's home on Kaua'i, where, according to Izzy, Sam had fallen in love with shave ice and was trying to convince Henry to open a stand in Thunder Ridge upon their return.

Unlocking the door that opened to a storage area, Derek said, "Here we are," his voice sounding overly loud in the empty restaurant. He stepped back, allowing Willa to enter first. Knowing exactly where to find the light, she clicked it on, then led the way into the kitchen. The aromas of deli fare—potato and fried-onion knishes, corned beef, all the yummy comfort food—teased her nose as if the deli was open and ready for business, and she realized how hungry she was. "Octavio must have been cooking ahead for next week," she surmised. Why else would a restaurant that had been closed for a couple of hours smell like it was in the middle of a dinner rush? "I wonder if they're catering something?" Usually when the Pickle Jar catered, Izzy tapped Willa for cakes and cookies, but no one had mentioned an upcoming event.

"I don't know," Derek said, "but it's making me hungry. I haven't had dinner."

"Me, either." She glanced over. A smile (truly adorable, let's be honest), played at the corners of his mouth. She began to imagine a private picnic in the closed restaurant. Raiding the walk-in refrigerator and the adjacent bakery, lighting a candle and setting it on one of the tables or at the counter. Maybe she would say something like, "You've never had a cheese blintze with marmalade? You have to taste it" and use her fingers to pop a bite into his mouth.

Why not? Do it. Don't think. Just—

"You know," she ventured, interrupting her own thoughts before they talked her out of it, "if we're both hungry, we're in the right place." Her heart pounded with every word. "I bet we could find something to—"

"Surprise!"

Willa squealed as dozens of familiar people popped out from behind booths and tables in The Pickle Jar's dining room.

A hand reached out to steady her. A big, warm, supportive hand. Derek leaned close. "Happy birthday, Willa."

His calm murmur tickled the hair by her ear and sent shivers all the way through her. It took several seconds to find her voice. "This is for me?"

His smile gentled. "All for you."

Willa turned toward the crowd of people who were calling out, "Happy birthday!" and asking Derek, "Is she surprised?"

As her gaze roved around the crowd, she noted Izzy, along with Nate and their son, Eli; Holliday Bailey, the librarian; Kim, her coworker from the bakery, who was holding hands with her husband; and a good thirty other people. Standing in front of them all, holding a hand-lettered poster that shouted Happy Birthday, Willa/Teacher! was Gilberto. His grin held none of the shyness it had when they'd first met, the afternoon he'd decided to take the donation jar. Instead, he looked excited, full of importance in a really good way.

Derek placed a hand on the small of her back, gently urging her forward.

As she moved from the kitchen to the dining counter, around which most of the guests were crowded, Willa became aware that the chattering and greetings were becoming more subdued until they quieted altogether. Dozens of faces looked at her expectantly, making her acutely conscious that of all the folks here to celebrate her birthday, to celebrate *her*, she didn't know any of them very well, and they knew her…hardly at all. Not a one of them would be able to name the most important events of her life; that's how she had wanted it. Now her reluctance to let these people into her world made her feel awkward and kind of small as they waited for her to say something.

"Thank you," she started off breathlessly. "This is such

a surprise." *Duh.* "I mean, I truly, truly had no idea. I can't believe you went to all this trouble." She shook her head, shocked when tears began to prick her eyes. "I'm speechless," she concluded lamely.

Her relief was great when Derek took over. "Somebody said there'd be food at this shindig," he called out. "The birthday girl hasn't had dinner. Let's eat!" Enthusiastic applause traveled around the restaurant.

Izzy and Octavio—it looked as if the entire staff had given up their night off for her—sprang into action. Out came the platters of food whose aromas had enticed her as soon as she'd opened the door. A line formed at the counter, and plates were filled. Several people greeted Willa personally and urged her to eat. She promised to join everyone in a moment, but she wanted to talk to Gilberto first.

"You made that sign?" She pointed to the large electric-yellow poster board he held.

Nodding, he boasted, "I spelled everything right, too. Do you like it?"

"I love it. Thank you. And thank you for spending your Friday with me. I know you usually watch a movie with your cousins on Fridays."

His gaze shifted. "We don't do that so much anymore."

She frowned. He'd only told her about his busy Friday nights two weeks ago. *"Me and my cousins do a lot of fun stuff,"* he'd said.

"Well, people have busy seasons sometimes," she reasoned. "Schedules can change temporarily."

Gilberto shrugged, but some of his joy seemed to evaporate.

"If you're free tomorrow," she said spontaneously, "there's a theater in Portland that plays reruns. They're showing *Hotel Transylvania*, one and two. I love those movies. And there's an ice cream store nearby that's serving Vampire Blood ice cream and another flavor called Creepy Cake Batter, which has actual bug brittle in it. That's a crunchy candy with pieces of real bugs. I dare you to taste it."

Gilberto screwed up his face. "Gross! I'll taste it if you will."

Willa laughed. "I'll decide after the movie."

"Did I hear someone mention ice cream?" Derek appeared beside them, making Willa's skin tingle from the nearness.

"Bug ice cream," Gilberto crowed, socking Derek on the arm. "Willa dared me to eat some."

As he chattered on about the kinds of bugs he imagined would be in the ice cream, Willa realized she envied Gilberto's easy way with Derek.

"*Mi abuela* grew up eating a dish called *sompopos* in Guatemala," Derek said when Gilberto dared *him* to eat an insect. "*Sompopos* are ants. She cooked them in butter."

"No way!" Gilberto found this fascinating.

Actually, so did Willa. "You're Guatemalan?"

"My grandmother was mestiza, half Indian and half Spanish. Her daughter, my mother, married an Irish lad."

"Guatemalan," Willa mused. "Is that the reason for your year-round tan?" She touched his wrist—a purely unconscious gesture that, paradoxically, made her hyperconscious of, oh boy, everything about him. Conscious of the hair on his arm and the smoothness of the skin beneath. Conscious of the scent beneath his clean-soap smell and the subtle aftershave he wore. The scent she most often associated with Derek was just him. Warm, comforting, enticing, stirring… Derek.

He glanced to her fingers, resting light as butterflies on his wrist. His gaze seemed to electrify their touch, but when his brow lowered, she pulled away self-consciously.

Derek's big hand clamped onto Gilberto's shoulder. "Grab some food and a booth. We'll be right behind you."

Gilberto didn't require a second invitation to eat. Presenting the Happy Birthday sign to Willa, he jumped into the buffet line, where several people pushed him on ahead of them, making sure his plate was piled.

"He really is becoming part of the community," Willa observed softly, looking up at Derek to find him watching her steadily. He relieved her of the large cardboard sign, tucking it behind a stool at the counter, then returned to her. Derek stood a good ten inches taller than she, and she felt at a slight disadvantage. "I'm guessing my car is actually okay?"

"It's fine. I'll take you back to get it in the morning. Or tonight, if you need it."

More time alone with him sounded good to her, or it would if she didn't sense the distance between them.

"It was incredibly good of you to go to all the trouble you did to get me here." She surveyed the scene around them. Someone had added music to complete the party atmosphere, and for the first time she noticed the balloons. "I still can't believe Izzy organized this, as busy as she is."

"She's capable of it, but it wasn't Izzy," Derek said. "It was Gilberto's idea. Izzy was all for it." He stopped, shaking his head. "Actually, she was a little concerned you might feel uncomfortable with the attention, but Gilberto insisted."

"Gilberto did?"

"He heard Izzy mention your birthday and came to me so fired up to throw you a party, I couldn't have talked him out of it if I'd tried."

"He came to you." She frowned. "That means *you* planned this?"

"Gilberto planned. I facilitated." Derek crossed his arms

in the classic sheriff stance she was starting to find more endearing than intimidating. "I'm not big on parties, but he's right. You deserve one."

The word "deserve" deepened her frown. "I haven't done anything to deserve all this—"

He silenced her by pressing his index finger to her lips, and if touching his wrist was electrifying, that was nothing compared to the pad of his finger on her lips.

"You're important." His voice was husky, heavy. "To this town. To Gilberto." His eyes, deep and dark and burning like the core of a volcano, told her what he didn't say out loud. *To me. You're important to me.*

"I thought you didn't like me anymore." Though she attempted to say it ironically, Willa heard the faint pleading tone that turned her statement into a question. She cringed inwardly, wanting to take the words back, but Derek's lips curved in the most mesmerizing quarter smile.

"That would be way, way too easy." He wagged his head. "And so far nothing with you has been easy."

"I know. I'm sorry."

"Don't be." After a moment of what appeared to be an internal battle, he announced, "I'm driving you home tonight after the party. Could your car use an oil change?"

She nodded.

"Dan Bowman will take care of it and bring your car over in the morning."

Done. His tone said not to argue. A thrill shivered up her arms.

"Okay, you two, time to hit the buffet." Izzy slapped Derek on the shoulder—rather hard, Willa thought. "You're monopolizing the birthday girl. Let her eat and mingle."

Derek glowered at Izzy. Willa smiled at the knowledge that he really did want to spend more time with her. Even as she slipped into the buffet line ahead of Derek, she imagined inviting him into her home later that night. Anticipation rose, and she felt like one of the sparkling cider bottles Jax Stewart was opening at the beverage table. Any more internal pressure, and she'd bubble up all over the place.

No. That was way too tame a comparison. She didn't feel like a bottle of apple cider; she felt like a woman who knew exactly what she wanted. And what she wanted was Sheriff Derek Neel—out of uniform, thank you very much.

A millisecond after that thought, his hand settled on her waist, and lust erupted inside her, like a long-lost friend she hadn't expected to see again. *Turn around. Let him know what you're feeling. That's how this is done.*

She looked behind her, and the moment they made eye contact the inferno spread, heating the space between them. Suddenly Willa was ravenous, but not for dinner. The feeling was frightening and exhilarating and wonderful.

"Knish?" A Pickle Jar employee stood behind the counter, a smile on her pretty, young face, and a fat square pocket of golden dough balanced on the spatula she held out. "Happy Birthday, Willa," she said brightly. "I'm so glad I could come tonight. Do you want meat or potato?" She nodded to the knish.

Derek's hand fell away, leaving a void that acted like a rush of cold wind to cool Willa down. She answered the question then struggled to make small talk. When she glanced at Derek again, he was listening to Ray, the barber, complain about the new construction in town wrecking the "legitimate authenticity of original structures."

Derek looked over at Willa, his expression impassive. He gave her one slow wink. It was all she needed to begin counting the minutes until her birthday party was over and the main event of the evening began.

Chapter Eight

The full moon peered down from behind a misty cloud cover as Derek helped Willa out of his squad car. Foggy breath mingled and hovered between them under the old-fashioned iron street lamp as the evening's first fat flakes of snow began to float to the ground.

When Willa tilted her face up, Derek caught the child-like wonder in her smile. "I never get tired of the snow," she said. "We haven't had enough."

"That's unusual around here." Ordinarily he thought an inch or two of snow was plenty, but seeing her expression and the flakes of snow that clung to her hair could make him revise his opinion. "Some years, we'd be up to our ankles in it by now."

Together, they stood on her sidewalk, watching the snow begin to dance and swirl around them in the circle of lamp-light. The happy, relaxed sound of Willa's sigh burrowed into Derek's heart.

"Really, I don't mind going out and getting my car," she offered. "We should probably do it, before the streets get super slick."

And end this moment? "Nope. It's late, and you don't have snow tires. Besides Dan Bowman really wants to throw in a lube job. He'll have your car here first thing in the morning. It's his birthday present."

"You've gotta love a small town." A poignant smile made her face shine. "I can't thank you enough for throwing me such a wonderful birthday party."

"You're welcome. I'm glad you had a good time. Gilberto was so happy that we actually managed to surprise you, he told me he's going to throw parties for a living." They'd dropped the boy off at his cousin's house before heading to Willa's, and he'd jabbered the entire way.

Willa giggled, the first time he'd heard that particular sound from her. "I know." She nodded. "He was so excited and so full of sugar, I wonder if he'll sleep a wink tonight."

Derek touched a snowflake that landed on the tip of her nose. It was all he could do to keep from threading his fingers through her gorgeous red waves. "How about you?" His murmur produced another puff of cloudy breath. "Are you tired?"

Her eyes were wide, her smile knowing and somewhat shy when she assured him, "No. Not a bit."

He took her elbow, and they headed up her porch steps.

Willa's home was one of the post-WWII cottages that were typical in this area, with a steeply pitched roof and a wide porch that spanned the front and two sides of her house. Matching wooden keg planters with large winter cabbages and a few hardy pansies in purple flanked her front door. The taupe-color siding appeared to have been recently painted, as did the black shutters framing the windows. Off to one side a two-seater swing hung from the porch's ceiling, and beside it, at first glance Derek thought he spied a bronze floor lamp. Closer inspection revealed that it was the kind of outdoor propane heater used to warm restaurant patios.

He gestured in its direction. "You use this thing much?"

"All the time."

"This time of year?"

"Especially this time of year."

"You're kidding." He took several steps to better look it over.

"No. I love to see the stars on a clear night. Makes me feel closer to…" she shrugged and looked wistfully into the misty heavens. "Nature, I guess."

Derek watched her face angle toward the cloud-filtered moonlight. What did she see that drew such pensive thoughts?

Giving her head a shake, Willa stepped over to plug in a strand of star-shaped twinkle lights that rimmed the porch ceiling. "This is how I combat a cloudy day," she explained, switching on the propane heater. Suddenly, an orange light cast a pool of warmth, transforming her porch into a cozy room. "Hang on a minute," she said, a mischievous note in her voice as she unlocked her front door.

Since he wasn't invited inside, Derek used his time unobserved to glance around the porch. Noting homey touches that spoke of the hours she spent here, he walked over to examine a forgotten book that sat on a small table next to the swing. He picked up the slim hardcover, running his thumb across the title. *Coming Back from Grief.* A bookmark stuck out one third of the way into the pages.

It didn't take a private investigator to understand that Willa was trying to heal. But from what? Replacing her reading material, he ambled to the opposite end of the porch and looked out across the street, his mood taking a sharp downturn. Would she ever feel safe enough to confide in him? He suspected some of the answers to the Willa puzzle were inside the house. Is that why she hadn't invited him in? Briefly, he thought about following her inside, but before he could act, Willa reappeared carrying two beach towels and a large Pendleton blanket.

The unspoken invitation to stay softened his sudden grumpiness. "Beach towels?" he asked. "In the middle of winter?"

"Feel," she invited, holding the pile out to him.

"They're warm."

"I keep them hanging on a quilt stand in front of the radiator."

After she'd arranged the towels on the plump outdoor swing cushions, she sat and gestured for him to join her under the toasty wool blanket.

The swing creaked as they settled on it.

Tucking the warm blanket all around their shoulders, Derek deliberately pressed his thigh against hers. She didn't move away. In fact, she leaned against his arm as she arranged the blanket over their laps.

Derek arched a brow at her. "So this is what it means to be snug as a bug in a rug."

"Yup. Magical, isn't it?"

"Pretty much, yeah." Illuminated by the heat lamp and twinkle lights, Willa's skin glowed, as smooth and creamy as peach ice cream, and her eyes sparkled with enjoyment, for once undisturbed by shadows from the past. "You're magical."

To his own ears, Derek's voice sounded as thick and warm as the wool that wrapped them both in one cocoon.

Beneath the cover, he reached for her hand, threading his fingers through hers. Her smile deepened. All along his left side, their bodies touched. The snow was swirling out of the sky with increasing gusto, coating her lawn and the grove of trees across the street. The weatherman's report that Derek had seen earlier said they'd get five or six inches tonight. He was glad she wouldn't be out driving in it. The first day of real snowfall each year equaled fender benders and worse. Before morning, he would no doubt get a call or two requiring him to lend a hand directing traffic around someone in a ditch.

For the time being, he didn't want to think about that. Didn't want to think about going anywhere. This was perfect.

Around them, the world fell silent except for the dulcet hum of the heater, and off in the distance a train whistle sounded its haunting song. The train's rumble gently vibrated the floorboards.

Slowly, Derek reached out from under the blanket to pull a snow-dampened strand of hair away from her cheek and lower lip. He'd been dreaming about her every damned night for a year. He inhaled as his desire for her surged.

Easy now. Take it slow.

The muscles in his jaw worked with the effort it took to relax.

A sigh, so light that only her misty breath told him he hadn't imagined it, made him lean closer. His resolve crumbled like the walls of Jericho. She was completely intoxicating. Giving into the heady rush of adrenaline that rocketed through his gut, he released the fingers he held beneath the blanket, cupped her jaw in his hands and pulled her mouth firmly beneath his.

He'd promised himself that tonight would be his very last attempt to woo her. Yeah, he'd said it before, but this time… If she rebuffed him now, he would force himself to move on in spite of the fact that he was pretty convinced this woman was his destiny.

Immediately Derek sensed this kiss was different—hotter and more urgent than the others had been. Relief flooded every cell as she kissed him back with the same passion he felt, and soon, like a door opening on a flaming backdraft, they were consumed. Cold noses, warm lips and tongues, their lungs laboring—it felt to him as if they had stopped being two distinct individuals and instead were one heart pounding with want. With need.

One kiss became two, then three. Derek took Willa into his embrace, her lower back resting against his lap, her shoulders cradled in his arms. Their kisses gave way to guttural whispers shared in the hushed snowfall.

"I haven't made things easy on you, have I?" She stared up at him.

"Hell, no."

Willa traced his lips with gentle fingers, which nearly drove him mad. "I'm sorry."

He kissed the tip of her nose, her jaw and an apparently sensitive spot beneath her ear. "You're forgiven."

She looped her arms around his neck. "Thank you for hanging in there with me. You know, for being so patient and persistent."

"You're worth the wait."

"You, too."

Derek allowed himself to bask in this victory. Pulling her more firmly against his chest, he murmured against her hair. "I could sit here like this forever."

Willa leaned back, pressing her lips together. "I'm not so sure about forever."

"Too cold, huh?"

"It's just that I'm more about being in the moment."

Uh oh. Derek took a deep breath and held it. Was she erecting barriers again?

As if he were trying to capture a bird poised to fly, he

locked his fingers behind her back. "Are you making small talk or trying to tell me something?"

Her sigh was heavy, underscored by a barely audible moan. She plucked at a bright red thread of wool hanging loose on their blanket. "The whole 'forever' thing… I just don't believe in that."

"Do you trust me enough to tell me why?"

"It's me I don't trust, not you." She was still cradled in his lap. Warm and soft and utterly right in his arms, a position definitely to her advantage when she ran her fingers across the stubble on his cheek and asked, "Do you really want to stop what we're doing to have a philosophical conversation? Does 'why' matter tonight?"

It mattered. But he knew the conversation wouldn't change anything in this moment.

Beyond them, the world was now covered in a downy comforter of sparkling white. A clean slate. Derek knew the presence of the grief books and someone in her not-too-distant past held the answers she was reluctant to give. Did she have a new beginning left in her heart, in spite of her words to the contrary? Her kisses promised so much more than she would admit.

"Anyway," she said, "This…what we have here…we should let it be what it is."

"What do you think it is?"

"It's wonderful. And temporary."

"An affair."

She wrinkled her nose. "That sounds tawdry."

Actually, his blood heated at the image, but as he kissed her again, he couldn't quite bring himself to believe she meant it.

As if she could read his mind, she admonished breathlessly, "I'm serious. This won't ever lead anywhere permanent."

"Okay." He nodded solemnly. "Of course, it's your loss. You said yourself I'd make a great dad someday."

"You will. You do." She spoke carefully. "But not with me as the mom."

She was watching him, waiting for him to show that he understood. Which he sure as hell did not, because everything—every little thing—he knew about her said *love, family, forever.* But for now he decided to give her what she was looking for, because there was so much more to discover. "All right, Willa. We'll play by your rules. For the time being," he murmured, hauling her closer for several more kisses, meant to distract. When she was breathless, he asked, "So this affair. Care to elaborate?"

Looking beautifully mussed and a bit dazed, she shook her head. "No. Just the standard, exciting, clandestine, secret, middle-of-the-night rendezvous will do."

"Secret, huh? Will I have to climb out of your window, or will you allow me to use the front door? Or, are you planning to keep this affair of ours confined to the front porch?"

Her mood lifted once more, and her giggle rocked the swing. "Definitely not the front porch. Remember, my neighbor Belleruth is an insomniac. If she saw us, the entire block would hear about it before breakfast."

"Small town. Big talk." He massaged her back. "Can't have that." Though he couldn't have cared less.

"No," she whispered against his mouth. "We can't have that. Myra at Hair Today would start some under-the-hair-dryer gossip that would spread to the *Tribune* by the end of the week."

"Okay then. A tawdry affair it is." He kissed her until he was pretty sure she'd have trouble stringing together the words to make a sentence.

Then, just as she was completely limp in his arms,

Derek marshaled every ounce of strength in his nearly two-hundred-pound body and lifted them both to their feet. "Good night, Willa."

The slack-jawed expression she wore on her face was priceless. Clearly, she expected their affair to begin that night. But Derek wasn't in this thing for short-term success. He was in it to win it.

"Since every tawdry affair should begin with a real date," he told her, "I'll pick you up tomorrow night at six. Hooligans. Dinner, dancing. Dress accordingly."

And with that he strode, whistling into the dark, to his car.

He left? Stunned, Willa stood, staring at the tracks Derek's tires left in the pristine snow. A minute ago, she'd thought they were really headed somewhere. Specifically, her bedroom. And then?

He'd up and left. Just like that, leaving her heart hotly pounding blood through her veins with no avenue of release. Mind whirling, she gathered the blanket and towels and stepped inside her house, closing the front door behind her.

Surely, she'd made herself clear. She didn't need to be wined and dined. They could dispense with the whole getting-to-know-the-real-you process.

She did not want strings. Ties. Knots in her stomach.

Ties could bring love, and love eventually brought sorrow. And Willa had sorrowed enough for one lifetime. Slowly, she folded her blanket and towels over the quilt stand and crossed to the mantel of her fireplace.

"Hey," she whispered to a framed photograph, tracing the face she found there with her fingertip. "What would you have me do?"

As Willa pondered the lively, sparkling eyes that looked at her with such adoration, she began to sense the answer.

"But am I ready?" she whispered. "I know it's been two years, but I'm just so—" her sigh clouded the glass "—so very tired."

She scrubbed the fog with the tip of her finger so that the eternally smiling eyes came back into focus, ever encouraging.

"I don't think I can," she admitted. "Missing you has used me up."

The expression in the photograph would never change. As long as she peered at the picture, she could slip, if only for a twinkling, into that glorious time when love had been mostly pain-free. Her memories lent her the encouragement to live again. But to love?

Picking up the frame, she cradled it in her arms and headed to bed.

As Derek rounded the corner to city hall, he spotted a lone figure shuffling along the sidewalk. The snow had started to come down something fierce, and though his wipers were set to high speed, he was having trouble seeing. This person was either a very small adult, or a child. Deciding to err on the side of caution, he slowly pulled up next to the pedestrian and rolled his window down.

"Everything all right?" he called.

The small person stopped and squinted into his headlights.

"Gilberto? Is that you? What the devil are you doing out here?" Derek glanced at his dashboard. "It's nearly eleven o'clock at night."

Shoulders hunched against the weather, Gilberto came around to the driver's side and poked his head inside the window. "I was looking for you."

"Well, you found me." Hitting the unlock button, Derek nodded toward the rear passenger door. "Hop in." Rather than climbing in the back, Gilberto wasted no time diving into shotgun position and pulling the door closed. "You eighty pounds?" Derek asked skeptically.

"You kidding me? I'm almost eighty-five!"

"My bad. Belt," Derek reminded him as he pulled back onto Ponderosa Avenue. Lucky thing he'd decided to make a quick sweep of the town before turning in for the night. "Wanna tell me what you think you're doing out for a stroll at this time of night in the middle of a snowstorm?"

"I didn't want to call 911."

"Why would you need to do that?"

"I didn't. That's why I was walking."

"Dude, help me out. Why *didn't* you need to dial 911?"

"Oh! Roddy and his friends were getting really drunk. Music was so loud, I couldn't sleep. So I go out to the living room to tell Roddy I can't sleep, and *Roddy* is sleeping. I couldn't wake him up, and his friends were all laughing and doing stuff to him."

"What kind of stuff?"

Gilberto made a valiant effort not to laugh, but failed. "One of 'em was putting lipstick on him and another guy was taking pictures. But when they wanted to do some of that crap to me? I was outta there, man."

Derek cut a glance over at the kid and nodded. "Did the right thing, buddy boy. But next time you might want to call me and have me come get you, instead of freezing half to death."

"I don't have your number."

As Derek reached for his radio he said, "We'll have to fix that, huh." Then, thumb to the talk button, he called, "Russell, you out there?"

Static crackled as Russell responded, "I'm here, dog. What can I do ya for?"

"I need you to run over to check on Gilberto's cousin." He gave the address. "I got a report that Roddy is passed out on the couch, but just in case it's more serious than that..."

"Ten-four. I'm leaving now."

"Great. While you're there, make sure Roddy knows Gilberto is with me, and see if the music needs to be turned down."

"I'm on it."

"Thanks. I'm out." He snapped his radio into its holder and glanced at Gilberto. "Wanna make some rounds with me?"

"You mean like a deputy?" The boy's obsidian eyes shone in the dark.

"Just like a deputy."

"Hell, yeah!"

Given that he wanted to laugh, Derek directed toward his young passenger the sternest glance he could manage. "You mean heck yeah."

"Right!"

"Good. When we're done, we'll head to my place. You can spend the night at my ranch."

"That would be awesome! So, you live on a ranch? Do you have cows?"

"No. But I have several horses. You can help me feed them in the morning."

Gilberto pumped his fists, not the least bit tired. "Yes!"

"You hungry?"

"Totally."

"Figures." He'd eaten plenty at dinner, but Derek remembered his own predilection for consuming as much as possible at that age. "Okay. Since it's the weekend—and only because it's the weekend—you can stay up late. I'll make you an early breakfast when we get home."

"Oh, man, this is turning out to be the best night ever."

Smiling, Derek wagged his head. The kid was easy to please. He thought about what he'd started on Willa's porch, about the fact that he was going to see her the next day, and about how much he enjoyed the company of the eleven-year-old beside him. He wasn't thrilled about Roddy's behavior, not one little bit. Nonetheless, he was inclined to agree: this was a pretty good night indeed.

Chapter Nine

"Is that Gilberto in the backseat of your truck?" Willa asked Derek as the grinning child hung out the window and waved at her. From where she and Derek stood on her front porch, she lifted a hand to wave back then shot a quizzical glance at the man beside her. Didn't they have a dancing date right about now?

"Yeah. That's him," he confirmed. "There's been a slight change of plans. A little more than slight."

Willa's face crumpled with disappointment and she instantly felt foolish. "Oh." She strove to find a blithe recovery. "That's okay. Really. Another time, then?"

He looked confused. "What? No, no, I want to spend the evening with you. I mean, if *you* still want to. But it's going to be a group date…type…thing." He dragged a hand through his hair. "The kid's bunking with me for a couple of days."

Along with surprise, Willa felt a frisson of alarm. "Is he in some kind of trouble?"

"No." He took a moment to explain how he'd found Gilberto on the road. "You remember his cousin Roddy?"

"Who could forget?" Roddy's belligerence at their meeting left a strong impression.

"He ended up in the hospital with a pretty serious case of alcohol poisoning. Some of the other party animals were booked with MIPs."

"What's that?"

"Minor in possession. Roddy was playing bartender and some of his patrons were underage. Needless to say, Roddy had a little visit by DHS this morning. The caseworker informed him that she decided to remove Gilberto from his custody temporarily until they can investigate Roddy's ability to provide safe care. So, I've got the kid until further notice."

Willa was instantly sympathetic. "He's so lucky he has you. You stepped right up to the plate."

Derek obviously wanted to shrug away her praise. "Yeah, well, we didn't really have much choice. The closest DHS office is closed today, and I have a foster care certification. We're going to play the next few days by ear."

"Why are you certified to do foster care?"

"I have been since I started the job. Walt was certified and suggested I do it, too. Said you never know when you're going to make a difference in someone's life. I maintain the license every year, but I've never needed it before. Anyway, when I told Gilberto that I was supposed to have dinner with you, he came up with a pretty cool idea. Unfortunately, as much as I hate to say it, you might want to change out of that knock-out dress and into something more suited to the great outdoors."

Willa swallowed her disappointment. On her lunch hour that day, she'd bought a sexy new dress just for the occasion. And the appreciative look currently in Derek's eyes made it worth every penny of the exorbitant price she'd paid. Counting the seconds until he'd arrived, she'd even braved her front porch with her coat over her arm instead of snugly around her. "Why don't you and Gilberto come in while I change?"

She caught the surprise that crossed his face before he turned and gestured to Gilberto.

"You might want to think ski gear," he suggested as she opened her door.

"We're going skiing?" No wonder he looked like an ad for the local Summit Lodge mountain resort, in a chocolate cable-knit sweater that gorgeously accented his tanned skin.

"Not skiing, exactly. But I think you'll enjoy yourself. Gilberto and I put our heads together and...well, you'll see. I would have called to tell you about the change in plans—I should have called you—but I didn't want you to change your mind."

"I wouldn't have."

The small, pleased quirk of Derek's lips gave her goosebumps.

"You got a swing!" Gilberto's voice rang from outside Willa's front door. His face popped into view. "Can I swing on it?"

"Sure," she laughed. Being around Gilberto had reintroduced her to the irrepressible energy of childhood. It had been a long time since she'd experienced it up close and personal. "Close the front door if you're staying outside, though, okay?"

"Yep."

He did as requested, and a moment later the creak of the thick chains holding the swing was audible as he sat. Willa shook her head. "I forgot that the simplest things are often the most entertaining when you're young."

When she looked at Derek, he was studying the fireplace mantel. Instantly, her heart began to hammer. She had removed the photo last night, hadn't she? Scanning the heavy oak shelf, she saw a picture of herself and Daisy Dunnigan on a trip to New York, and a photo of her parents together in Paris for their thirtieth anniversary. Other than that, the mantel held only her small collection of candlesticks.

Relief flooded her. Time with Derek was meant to be an escape. She wasn't ready for questions that would jerk her back into the past.

"I'm going to change. It'll just be a minute." Heading to the bedroom, she rummaged through her dresser for a heavy sweater and her Lycra ski pants. She shimmied out of her dress and pantyhose and into a pair of pink long johns and heavy socks. Not quite the seductive effect she'd been shooting toward, but it would have to do. He was a rare man in this day and age, this sheriff of hers, putting the needs of a child who wasn't even his above his own desires. He knew how to look at life in the long run.

In just a couple of minutes, she'd shed her earrings, pulled on her ski clothes and tamed the static electricity in her hair.

"So, will you take a rain check on the dancing?" Derek called from her living room.

Willa grinned at her reflection in the mirror and nearly didn't recognize herself. The woman smiling back looked both excited and happy. "Of course."

"And..." He drew out the word, an interesting note in his voice. "Will you wear that dress for me again?"

Laughter rose into her throat. She glanced at the clingy jade-colored wraparound she'd tossed onto her bed. "You like that dress, hmm?"

"*Ohhhh*, yeah."

When, she wondered, was the last time she felt this good? "I'm almost done. Just tying my boots. Would you mind grabbing my ski jacket from the hall closet? Next to the front door." When she came out of her bedroom, Derek helped her into her jacket. A pair of gloves, a hat and a scarf from a drawer in the entry credenza were the last touches. "Ready," she finally announced.

"Not just yet." Reaching for the ends of her scarf, Derek drew her close for a kiss that instantly had her blood boiling and wanting to shed her down jacket. "I can't do that in front of the kid," he murmured. "And I didn't want to wait."

"I like the way you think, Sheriff Neel." Her voice emerged husky and flirtatious. Her heart began to thrum so hard, she could actually hear it and wondered if he could, too. Oh, how she wished they could stay here tonight.

As things were getting interesting, Gilberto pounded on the front door. "We should go now!"

"Gilberto is a little excited," she observed wryly.

"Not as excited as I am," Derek groaned, dropping one more kiss on her waiting lips. Gilberto tried the knob then rang the bell. "I'm glad that door was locked."

Once they were all on the road, Gilberto regaled her with the tales of last evening. "I was a real deputy. I got to wear a badge. Right here." He thrust his skinny chest between their seats and pointed to the spot just above his heart.

"Belt on," Derek commanded.

"Okay, right! And then," he continued as he dropped back into his seat, "we went home and ate breakfast in the middle of the night. And this morning I fed Derek's horses. When you hold out a carrot, they eat it out of your hand. But they don't bite you or nothing."

"Anything," Willa and Derek chimed.

"Okay. They just go like this." He demonstrated. "Their lips are soft and fat and have sharp hairs."

While Gilberto waxed on in the backseat, Derek reached over and took Willa's hand. "They just go like this." He brought her hand to his mouth and oh-so-gently nibbled the palm.

Pleasure filled her. *Oh, good golly.* "That's how they do it, hmm?"

"Hey!" Gilberto called. "What are you guys doing?"

"Just showing Willa how the horse eats," Derek said.

"Oh." And Gilberto talked nonstop the rest of the way to the ranch.

Derek's place was only about fifteen minutes south of Thunder Ridge, but the snow made the going a little slower. When they turned down his long driveway, Willa spotted a charming log home nestled in a grove of giant fir trees. To the left of the house stood a stable and paddock. Immediately behind Derek's home was a snow-covered hill adorned with two rows of flaming tiki torches. The entire scene was a Thomas Kinkade painting come to life. Willa felt her pulse accelerate in a way it hadn't since she was a child.

Unable to control her giddy grin, she glanced quickly between Gilberto and Derek. "What on earth is this?"

"It's cosmic sledding," Gilberto informed, looking mighty pleased.

"Or our version of cosmic sledding, anyway," Derek said, returning her grin. "We don't have the big slides and colored lights, but we did our best."

As they pulled nearer the hill, Willa could see myriad trails had already been blazed between the torches and the snow between them was packed hard. Unbridled glee rose in her throat, making her voice squeaky. "We're going sledding?"

"Yes." Gilberto flung his seatbelt off. "We're gonna let the horse pull us to the top of the hill, and then we're gonna ride our sleds down. We already tried it out, and it's pretty cool."

Making eye contact with Willa, Derek arched a brow suggestively. "I can think of one or two things that might be better, but it *is* a total blast."

Willa couldn't stem the grin that felt as if it swallowed her entire face.

"We thought we'd sled for a bit and work up an appetite, before we head inside for some grub."

"We made barbecued chickens," Gilberto announced, opening the car door as Derek came to a stop in front of his house.

"I'm no chef like you," Derek told her, "but I figured you probably like to have someone else do the cooking once in a while."

"Is that what smells so wonderful?" Willa's mouth began to water as they got out of the car. The scent of mesquite and barbecue sauce was unmistakable. "Are you cooking outdoors?"

"Yep. Treated myself to a Traeger grill last Christmas."

She inhaled deeply. "Mmm. I smell sage. And rosemary."

He chuckled. "You're good. The chicken should be ready in about an hour. Till then, go with Gilberto to choose a sled, and I'll harness Autumn."

Once she and Gilberto had trudged to the bottom of the hill, Willa turned to take in the view of Derek's spectacular property in the waning twilight. His log cabin had huge mountain-facing windows that extended from the first floor all the way up to the peak of the second floor.

Indoor lamps cast pools of golden light through the glass and onto the snowpack below, and the entire forested countryside was awash in moonlight. Icicles clung to the eves spanning his rustic front porch, and smoke snaked from the river rock chimney. Willa could easily imagine enjoying this view with a cup of coffee first thing in the morning in one of the several rockers that flanked the living room windows.

Gilberto was already in the sled, making *shooshing* sounds as he pretended to be on a thrilling slide down the slopes. In response to the fun he was already having, Willa felt a rush of pure joy moments before guilt whomped her in the solar plexus with the force of a wrecking ball—not because she was at Derek's or planning to go sledding, but because for a moment she'd felt *only* happiness and anticipation. She'd just taken a giant step into a future that was hers. Hers alone.

Steadying herself, she took one breath and then another, letting go of self-reproach, willing herself to stay in the moment.

"Everything okay?"

Lost in thought, she didn't notice Derek had come up behind her. Guiding the horse he called Autumn, he looked as if he'd stepped off a poster for a movie Western. His gaze was watchful, concerned. Autumn blew a noisy puff of air through her wide nostrils and shook her head till her bit jangled. Derek stroked the horse's forelock, his big, gentle hands obviously welcomed by the mare.

I'm with you, sister. She didn't want to crawl back to the cave in which she'd been living the past couple of years. It was a nicely adorned cave, with windows to the outside world, but now that she truly had moved beyond its walls, she knew she couldn't retreat. Not yet, anyway, not while this man was standing right in front of her.

"Everything is fine." Smiling brightly, she joined Derek in petting the horse's broad forehead. "So this is Autumn," she said. "Glad to make your acquaintance." Derek had hitched a long toboggan to the horse's traces. "You going to tow us up that hill, girl?"

"She's ready if you're ready."

Willa was glad to see that his expression already had begun to relax. Rubbing her mitten-clad hands together, she nodded. "As I'll ever be, I guess. It looks a little scary."

"That's what makes it exciting." He stared at her, long and deep and mesmerizing. "I'm not going to let anything happen. To you or Gilberto. The thing about sledding is that to get a really good ride, you have to let go. Completely. Can you do that?"

She couldn't look away. "I can try."

"Good enough."

After some brief instruction by Derek on safety, she and Gilberto clambered aboard the long wooden toboggan behind him. Holding onto their sleds by ropes, they rode up the substantial incline to the crest. Impossibly, the view was even more stunning at the top. The twin rows of tiki torches glinted, beckoning them with the promise of adventure.

"C'mon, Willa, let's go," Gilberto urged, thrashing off toward the starting gate, his Flexible Flyer sled bobbing along behind.

Willa glanced at Derek. "It's a lot steeper than it looks from down there." Shadows flickered across the snow.

"It's not bad. Hang on tight, and you'll be fine. You steer this thing with your feet." He demonstrated on her sled as Gilberto took off down the hill on his, whooping with wild abandon. At her dubious expression, Derek laughed. "Come on, then. I'll go with you the first time." Tethering Autumn to a small tree, he positioned the sled, pulled Willa onto his lap and wrapped his arms around her waist. "You okay?"

"Yes. Now." And she was. Something about Derek's strong embrace made her fear evaporate. No wonder everyone seemed to trust the sheriff of Thunder Ridge, she mused as she looped her hands around his arms.

The air fled from her lungs as they took off after Gilberto. Giddy squeals filled her ears, and it took a moment before she realized they were coming from her mouth. *They were flying!* Rapidly they soared, up and over the occasional bump that tickled her stomach and stole her breath. The flames from the torches blended into an orange blur and all too soon they were at the bottom of the hill, plowing into a snow berm and panting with laughter.

Willa's face was nearly frozen, her nose dripping snow, and her wool hat sagging over her eyes. She felt *alive*, a feeling that was familiar and foreign and fantastic all at once. Pulling her to her feet, Derek straightened her hat, kissed the tip of her nose, then set off to get Autumn for a ride back to the top.

For over an hour Willa heard herself rivaling Gilberto's shrieks all the way down the hill, and then chatting over each other as the horse towed them back up. And, like the young boy, she was disappointed when Derek finally announced it was time to head inside and eat—although she had to admit, the aroma from his back deck had her stomach growling. Besides, it was snowing again and visibility was growing sketchy.

Caked with snow, her boots crunched along after Derek as he led Autumn to the stable. "You were right—that was so exciting! Much better than dancing."

Derek mock glared at her. "I'm going to take that as a challenge." Slipping an arm around her waist, he kissed her temple. "I'm glad you had a good time. I was looking forward to Hooligans, but I appreciate your going with the flow."

"Anytime you want to do this again, count me in."

"It was my idea," Gilberto announced, trudging up behind them. "Can I comb Autumn's hair with that one thing? You know?"

"Yup. Curry comb's in the tack room. Run ahead and open the stable door, sport."

They watched the preteen hike through the snow toward the sliding wooden door.

"He really seems to love it here. With you," Willa observed. She couldn't blame him. The ranch was a great place for a boy like Gilberto. And Derek… Derek was fun and funny and encouraging. A perfect role model. "Do you think he'll ever go back to live with Roddy?"

Derek's reply was swift and decisive. "I sure as hell hope not."

"Does he have other relatives he can live with?"

"I don't know. Doesn't sound like it. Sometimes DHS can dig up a distant relative who's willing to help."

"When they can't," Willa ventured, "what happens then?"

From the grim expression on Derek's face, Willa sensed that Derek had already begun to care pretty deeply for the child. "When no relatives are available, or capable, the state assumes guardianship."

"Foster care."

With one hand on the reins leading Autumn, Derek used the other hand to whip off his sodden wool cap and stuff it in his pocket. "We've got a long way to go before any permanent decisions are made." He shook his head at her. "This evening has been perfect so far. I don't want to worry about tomorrow's problems. And that's saying something for me."

Willa reached for his free hand and continued walking, a silent agreement to keep the night light.

Even so, as their boots and the horse's hooves stamped the snow and the tiki torches flickered on, she worried about the conscientious sheriff at her side. Because where Gilberto was concerned, Derek wasn't simply a sheriff taking care of a community matter. The boy's future had become personal to him. She saw the telltale signs of true affection, maybe even love. Without actually meaning to, she squeezed Derek's hand. Smiling crookedly, he squeezed back.

Please don't let him get hurt, she prayed. But even as she sent the prayer up, she knew it would be futile if he crossed the line from affection into love.

A blast of warm air greeted them as Derek held the kitchen door open for Willa and Gilberto. Immediately, Willa was in love. His kitchen was gorgeous. Knotty pine walls and cabinetry were the perfect backdrop for the chocolaty granite countertops and island. The appliances were state-of-the-art stainless steel; he even had an eight-burner stove that made her fingers twitch with the desire to grab a saucepan and start cooking. Beneath their feet, the hardwood floors were softened by colorful throw rugs.

"This is a beautiful remodel," she stated, knowing it couldn't be original to the house. "It should be on the cover of *Better Homes and Gardens*. Must have been a big project."

"The house deserved it. I had some money saved. Remodeling seemed like a good investment in the future."

A quiet *woof* punctuated his explanation, and Willa turned toward its source.

In one corner of the kitchen, an ancient dog, a shepherd

mix, lay on a bed in the corner, slapping the floor with his tail in greeting.

"Hey, Captain," Derek murmured as they walked over. He bent to scratch the grizzled head. Captain honored Derek with several kisses before he curiously eyed the new visitor. "Willa," Derek said, "this is Captain. He's about ninety in people years. He doesn't see too well anymore, so you always want to let him smell you before you touch him."

A dog lover her whole life, Willa extended her hand, grinning at the large twitchy nose that examined her thoroughly. At last, the old fellow decided she was kiss-worthy and licked her with the slowest, gentlest canine kiss she'd ever felt.

"What a lover," she cooed to him.

"Captain was named after Captain Hook in *Peter Pan*," Gilberto explained. "Tell her, Derek. Captain was a brave dude when he was younger."

"Later, sport. Why don't you two wash up at the sink and then, Gilberto, show Willa to the table while I rustle up the food."

"Can I help you?" Willa asked.

"Nope. Everything's under control. You relax."

"I want to light the candles." Already becoming familiar with Derek's house, Gilberto zoomed to the correct drawer to locate matches.

"Okay. Willa, make sure he doesn't set the house on fire."

Gilberto snorted. "Please, I'm eleven. I can light a match. Been doing it all my life."

"I hope not." Willa caught Derek's eye and returned his grin.

"Hey, I'm in the fifth grade."

"In that case, maybe Derek will let you drive me home tonight."

"Fifth graders aren't allowed to drive, but I could do it," Gilberto mused as he led Willa to the dining room. Tongue protruding slightly as he worked, he managed to light the match on the ninth or tenth strike. Soon, the candles on the table were flickering happily, lending a festive mood to the evening.

"You sure I can't help you?" Willa offered again as Derek moved back and forth from the deck and kitchen with mounds of food.

"Positive. You're our guest. Gilberto, help me with the dishes so Willa can relax."

While Gilberto willingly trotted behind Derek, Willa took the opportunity to make an exploratory stroll around the open-concept living and dining area. Much like the man who owned the house, the surroundings were ruggedly masculine, yet a woman would feel right at home here, too. Safe. Isolated from the outside world and its cares. Maybe that's what he meant when he'd said he'd remodeled with an eye toward the future—not merely that he was thinking about his investment, but that he wanted the ranch to be less a bachelor's retreat and more a family dwelling.

The living room was outfitted with large leather chairs and couches, covered with ivory and beige throws so soft they begged you to cuddle up. Hand-woven Indian blankets and artifacts adorned the walls, lending color and character. Soft music came from speakers in the polished wood ceiling, and built-in bookshelves bore evidence of a well-read owner. A fire crackled merrily in a river rock hearth.

Setting the last dish onto the farmhouse table that divided the kitchen from the living area, Derek called, "Dinner is served." Ravenous, Willa found her seat opposite him.

"I'm starving!" Gilberto announced as he watched Derek dish up a steaming plate of barbecued chicken, baked potatoes and savory roasted vegetables for Willa. "But I don't want any of that veggie stuff. I hate green junk."

"Fine. But, if you expect to get any of the dessert you ordered, green junk is on the menu." Derek's tone, though placid, brooked no argument, and Willa hid her smile behind her water glass. He really was a natural father figure. Someday, some lucky kid would no doubt reap the benefits.

Just…not with her.

Because the very idea threatened the cozy mood the evening had invoked, Willa pushed away all thoughts of tomorrow and simply allowed herself to revel in the delicious food and easy conversation. There were no lulls in said conversation, either. Gilberto treated them to an insane number of knock-knock jokes as they ate, and she and Derek laughed or groaned on cue. When they'd done justice to the meal, Gilberto moved into the kitchen to feed Captain a few remnants of barbecue that he'd saved from his plate.

"How did you end up living on a ranch?" Willa asked over a cup of after-dinner coffee.

Setting his napkin next to his plate, Derek leaned back in his chair. "Walt and his wife, Julie, weren't able to have kids. We became like family. When Walt was diagnosed with lung cancer, I was in the police academy, but came back to help. Julie had had heart surgery and wasn't doing well. When she passed, it took the wind out of Walt's sails. He went downhill pretty quickly."

"I'm—" Willa swallowed "—so sorry. I know how hard it is to lose someone you love." Eyes downcast, she twisted her napkin between her fingers, and blinked back the sudden, unwelcome urge to cry.

"Right before he passed, Walt claimed he was going to leave the acreage to his horses." Derek smiled wryly. "And the old codger actually did. But, there was an addendum that left the horses and everything they owned to me. And that's how I came to own a little piece of paradise."

"That's amazing," Willa murmured. "Walt sounds like he was a real character."

"He was. One in a million. Everybody in Thunder Ridge loved him. I figure..." Derek glanced over his shoulder at Gilberto, who lay on the dog bed with his arms around the snoring Captain. "I figure that Walt is the reason I give a damn about what happens to that kid."

Chapter Ten

"Dang." Gilberto sagged as yet another marshmallow fell off his stick in a flaming ball of goo. "Willa's come out way better than mine."

"She does seem to have the Midas touch, doesn't she?" Derek scowled at the black char on the end of his own skewer, adding another failure to their ever-growing discard pile.

Relaxed, happy and sated with food, Willa laughed at her two dinner companions. "*Now* are you willing to let me teach you how to make the perfect s'more?"

Together, they had cleared the dining table and settled onto a pile of pillows in front of the fireplace for dessert. Gilberto had lobbied to put s'mores on the night's menu, eager to try them for the very first time. Derek had loaded a tray with graham crackers, chocolate bars and a mountain of jumbo marshmallows, but so far the results were sketchy.

"I can't believe I need a lesson for this," Derek grumbled as he attempted, mostly in vain, to clean his metal skewer.

"Humility is the first ingredient in any successful recipe."

"You made that up."

"Not at all." Taking a sip of incredibly good coffee, Willa smiled. "In my former life, I taught at a culinary institute. The best chefs were invariably the ones who were the most teachable."

Derek's attention peaked. "Where was this culinary institute?"

"South Pasadena. I taught at Le Cordon Bleu," she shared. "It's not there anymore, unfortunately. I was also a pastry chef at a restaurant on Lake Boulevard."

"Lake Boulevard?"

"It's the South Pasadena equivalent of Rodeo Drive in Beverly Hills, or—" she paused to think "—Northwest Twenty-Third Avenue in Portland."

"Overly trendy and expensive?"

She laughed. "An epicurean's delight," she countered. "A hub for the most creative food in the city."

Pleasure filled Derek's face, and he nodded. "I like your confidence."

It was true: when it came to career, she'd rarely faltered.

"Confidence is very..." *S-e-x-y.* He mouthed the word, even though Gilberto was too involved in biting burnt marshmallow off his skewer to listen.

"Oh, I agree." Connection sizzled between them.

"So you had a great career," he observed. "Why did you leave?"

Crud. She'd walked right into that, and the answer was guaranteed to open the floodgates of her past. It would happen eventually, she knew, but she wanted to control when, where and how much she revealed. Tonight had been light and fun with moments of unexpected bliss. It had been, so far, much more than she'd expected. Discussing her past would change all that.

She shook her head. "I didn't leave. I'm still doing what I love, but now I'm doing it in Thunder Ridge. And I don't have to tell you why living in Thunder Ridge is so attractive."

She considered that an excellent save, but Derek's eyes narrowed. He knew she was hedging.

Curved around his skewer, his hands looked tense. Taking a chance, she covered his knuckles with her palm. "I like where I'm at right now, working in Thunder Ridge. Being here, with you and Gilberto. I loved today. And tonight has been perfect."

Let it stay that way, she implored silently, breathing a sigh of relief when his hand relaxed beneath hers.

"Rrrrrrgh." Gilberto's frustrated growl claimed their attention. He thrust his skewer at them. "I can't get it right. Willa, can you do mine?" he requested.

"Of course. I'll show you a few special tricks for the perfect s'more." She sent Derek a benevolent smile. "And may I say that the willingness to be taught shows true strength of character."

As she leaned forward to take Gilberto's stick, Derek whispered, "I'm going to remember you said that when it's time for me to show *you* a few special tricks."

His words filled her with a flush of anticipation. Quickly, she glanced at Gilberto, but he was busily engaged in choosing the perfect marshmallow for her to roast.

Ordering herself to focus on dessert, Willa cleared her throat. "Alrighty. Lesson one. Lightly—very lightly—warm your graham crackers and the chocolate to prepare them for the marshmallow."

"Prepare them. Check," Derek murmured.

Willa placed the crackers and chocolate in the metal grill basket Derek had bought especially for tonight and held it high over the flames. "We're not trying to toast these or melt the chocolate yet, remember. We're just getting them ready."

She jumped slightly as Derek's hand slid up her back. Softly, he kneaded the muscles at the base of her neck.

"What are you doing?" She sneaked the question out the side of her mouth.

"Getting ready." Smooth as silk, his voice matched the ministrations of his hand—soothing, confident, sexy. Willa's vision blurred a little.

"Now can we do the marshmallow?"

Gilberto's pleading question jerked her back to attention. "Right! So. You hold the marshmallow far enough away that the flame is just teasing it."

"That makes sense," Derek agreed in a tone that could only be called a purr. His fingers wandered to a spot—ooh, it was a very sensitive spot—below her right ear. "Only enough heat to tease..."

She closed her eyes for a second—honest to Pete, no more than a millisecond—until Gilberto shouted, "Look out!"

"Oops!" Willa yipped, laughing sheepishly as her marshmallow burst into flame.

"A little too hot for you there?" Derek goaded. To Gilberto he said, "She's demonstrating how *not* to do it, I guess."

"That's exactly right." Reaching for her own skewer, she jammed a fresh marshmallow onto the tip. "I allowed myself to get distracted. That's very bad."

Serenely, utterly serenely, she held the marshmallow over the flame, proud of how steady her hand was. "There.

See how it's light brown all over? That's what we're looking for. It's per-FECT!" Nearly shouting the second syllable, she sat bolt upright. Was that Derek's hand dipping below the waistband of her jeans?

While she sat there stupidly, doing absolutely nothing with the marshmallow, he let her go, took the skewer from her useless fingers and started to make the s'more for Gilberto exactly the way she had shown him. He presented it to the boy, who announced, "This is the best s'more ever."

"Isn't this your *first* s'more ever?"

"Yeah. It's the best."

Derek laughed.

He was acting as if nothing at all had happened. Several s'mores later, a few of which Gilberto proudly made on his own and served to them, Willa began to relax again.

"That's it for me. I pronounce you top chef," she told Gilberto, leaning back and holding her belly. "I'm retiring my skewer. I'm stuffed."

"Lightweight," Derek said good-naturedly as he, too, settled back.

"Hardly. I probably gained five pounds tonight."

"I don't see it. You'll have to show me where."

He was doing it again. Sounding innocent, but giving her a look that sent her blood pressure through the roof. She narrowed her eyes. This was definitely a game meant for two.

While Gilberto constructed yet another s'more, she took advantage of the unwitnessed moment. Scooting closer to Derek, she nudged his arm with her shoulder and reached for his hand. Instead of linking fingers, however, she drew her forefinger along his palm…his wrist… Then she curled her fingers under the sleeve of his sweater and explored his arm, loving the strength of it. When she felt his muscles tense and goose bumps cover his arm, she let a satisfied smile crease her face.

Now we're talkin'. She could feel the energy filling Derek's body and recognized the victorious sensation of her own sexual power. It had been ages.

"I don't want this s'more," Gilberto announced from his position in front of the fireplace. He plopped back on his heels. "I don't even know why I made it. I already ate, like, six."

"Uh oh." Willa sat up, pulling her hand away from Derek, but he refused to let go, sitting up with her. "I wasn't paying attention."

"Me, either." Derek thoughtfully studied the boy. "On the other hand, I don't think we have much to worry about. At least two of them are still on your face."

Gilberto probed the area around his mouth with his tongue.

"Why don't you head on upstairs and jump into the shower, since it's already past your bedtime. I'll be up to say good-night when you're done, okay?"

"Okay. What should I do with this?" Gilberto offered his latest creation to Derek. "Do you want it?"

"Nope. I can't eat another bite. It'll be too hard to eat by morning. You can toss it in the fire," he advised.

Gilberto looked affronted. "No, I don't want to burn it up. It's one of my best ones. This marshmallow is perfect. Look, Willa." He held it up for her to admire one last time. "Can I give it to Captain instead?

Derek shook his head. "Sorry. Chocolate is bad for Captain."

"It is?" Gilberto's brow creased with worry. "Why?"

Willa nodded. "Unfortunately, chocolate is poison to dogs."

Alarmed, Gilberto gasped. "Chocolate is *poison*?"

Derek chuckled. "Not to humans, bud." Having heard

his name, Captain limped in from the kitchen to nose his master's outstretched hand. "Hey, Captain. Did you hear us talking about you?" With happy grunts, the old dog curled up by Derek's side.

Gilberto watched his s'more go up in flames then leaned over to embrace the dog before he hugged Derek and Willa. "'Night, Captain. 'Night, Willa."

"Good night, buddy."

"Don't forget to brush your teeth," Derek ordered, "so they don't fall out after all that sugar."

"If they fall out, you've got to put money under my pillow, dude, so I'll believe in the tooth fairy. You don't want to, like, destroy my innocence or nothing."

Willa and Derek started laughing so hard, neither of them bothered to correct his grammar.

Clearly pleased to have received this reaction, Gilberto got to his feet, beaming. "You're both weird," he said contentedly, heading to a staircase constructed from split logs that had been polished to a soft golden sheen. Trailing his hand along the bannister, he called, "'Night, weirdos," from the landing and disappeared toward the room Derek had given him.

Turning to the man who still held her hand, Willa observed, "Considering he hasn't been here that long, Gilberto seems to have made himself right at home. You're good at this."

The muscles worked in Derek's jaw. "I suppose anything's better than bunking with Roddy and his idiot posse."

"Maybe, but don't sell yourself short. I barely recognize that boy from the one who was lurking in the bakery, trying to figure out how to steal. I wonder if Roddy wants him back?"

Derek's hand tightened on hers—unconsciously, Willa

guessed. "I don't know," he responded. "Gilberto doesn't talk about him much, but he's shared a couple of incidences that make me suspect longstanding neglect." His expression clouded. "Unfortunately family can become territorial. They may fight for their right to raise one of their own even when they're not committed to doing a good job of it."

Willa watched Derek's free hand gently stroke Captain's face and head. "If you had the option, would you be interested in becoming his foster parent?" she asked.

Derek thought for a long moment as on the other side of the wall of windows, the snow continued to fall. Occasional flurries swirled before being swept away by the whistling wind. Anticipating Derek's answer made Willa's stomach feel like those flurries. He was a born family man; anyone watching him with Gilberto would be able to see that. Of course, being good at something and being willing to do it every day, possibly for the rest of your life, were two different things. Did Derek have any idea what raising a child involved, far beyond the daily needs?

He inhaled long and deep, slowly exhaling before he answered her. "I try not to get too emotionally involved."

Unbidden, Willa's snort of laughter made Captain's tail thump on the floor. "I hate to break it to you, but you're already emotionally involved."

Derek appeared to be about to deny that, but his shoulders sagged. "Is it that obvious?"

Empathy welled as she smiled. "It's who you are. Caring. Sweet. Optimistic."

He tugged her close. "I'm no boy scout."

"In some ways you are. You're such a boy scout, you're a...a...*man* scout. People trust you. They're attracted to you."

"Right now, I'm only interested in whether one person is attracted to me."

She could feel the warmth from his skin. "Isn't it obvious?" she breathed. "I wouldn't be here if I wasn't attracted. Very."

They shared a kiss, each of them struggling with the self-control to make it last…and last. Willa expected to be interrupted by Gilberto, calling down that he was ready for bed, but, instead, Captain became the culprit. Hefting himself to his feet, he walked around until he was between her and Derek, forcing them to break apart. The old shepherd nosed Willa's hand until she reached out, weaving her fingers into the surprisingly soft fur.

Derek groaned in frustration. "I should have found you a different home when I had the chance."

"How could you say such a thing? Don't listen," Willa crooned in the old boy's ear. "He's just jealous."

"Damn straight."

As Willa scratched the dog's back, Captain lay down, swishing his tail across the floor.

"You like Willa, too, hmm?" Derek asked, and the dog crooned in delight, making her laugh. "He rarely trusts anyone this quickly."

"Really?" From upstairs, they could hear the sounds of Gilberto getting ready for bed. "What happened to Captain's paw?" she asked, referring to the strange-looking boot the dog wore below his right knee.

"He lost it in a trap."

"No!" She leaned in for a closer inspection of the Velcro and ripstop fabric sheath that secured a springy metal J-hook to his leg. "How horrible. Was it recently?"

"No, no. It happened about the same time Walt passed, so I guess it's getting close to a decade ago now. I was out one day, exercising one of the horses on an old forest-access logging trail up behind where we went sledding, and Stark, who has always been a pretty mellow horse, started acting real skittish. At first I thought maybe he'd picked up the scent of a bobcat or a bear, because we have plenty of those around here."

Willa watched his handsome face process the past in the firelight.

"After I got him settled down, I took a look around with my binoculars. Didn't see anything, but after a while, I heard a sort of high-pitched whine. Sounded like an animal was in pain."

"Captain." Willa murmured.

"Yeah."

You have a sad story, too, Willa thought as she gently stroked the intelligent face.

"Since I wasn't able to convince Stark to head toward the sound, I had to tether him and head into the woods on foot. Took me a while to locate him. I think he stopped moaning now and then as he heard me coming closer. Probably pretty afraid of me, too, right old man?" Derek's expression softened. He scratched a sweet spot just above the dog's tail.

"Anyway, I found him cowering on the ground, his paw caught in an illegal small-game trap. He was half starved to death and in obvious pain. He was real sweet as I released the trap, and let me tell you, trying to get that thing off him without doing more damage was tough. He whined more than once, but never tried to bite me."

Willa winced at the image of big-hearted Captain in a sawtooth trap.

"I took him into the local vet, but he couldn't save the paw. Together, though, we came up with a pretty cool prosthetic for him. We've refined it a few times over the years, but even in the beginning it wasn't too long before he was fat and sassy and off running around again, just like a pup."

"Wow. You are a lucky dog," Willa said to Captain.

Again, Willa was struck by how deeply Derek cared. Not only about Captain. About any underdog. "It's going to be so hard when he goes," she said, then realized how tactless that sounded. "I'm sorry. I didn't mean to say that out loud."

"No, it's okay. It's nothing I haven't already thought of. Or had to deal with before. I had another dog, back when I was in the police academy. When I adopted her, she followed me everywhere. People would laugh at me because I'd talk baby talk to her."

"Baby talk? Like?"

"You know. Things to build up her self-esteem."

"Ah. And she understood you?"

"Of course." Derek grinned.

"Adorable," Willa murmured. Like the man telling the story. "What were her favorite affirmations?"

"Nothing out of the ordinary. All the stuff a woman likes to hear." Both she and Derek were lying on their sides now, gazing at each other over Captain, who had lapsed into a soft snore. Derek ran the back of his finger ever-so-gently down Willa's cheek. "I'd tell her she was beautiful. And that failing puppy class did not make her a loser. She worried about that."

He has the softest, sweetest eyes I've ever seen. "Did she?"

"In weak moments. So I'd remind her that her struggles didn't define her." He spoke softly. "They made her stronger. More beautiful."

"I bet you say that to all the girls," she whispered back.

"No. Only to the strong, beautiful ones."

Willa felt as if she'd been in the desert for years, and Derek was a tall, cold glass of water. Every cell in her body drank him in. Thirsty for his touch, his kiss, she inched forward...

"I'm ready!"

Gilberto jumped down the stairs, swinging himself with both hands on the bannisters then crash landing three steps below where he'd started. "You can come up now."

As self-conscious as if she'd been caught buck naked, Willa sprang back.

Derek put a calming hand on her arm. "I'll be right up." To her, he said, "Can you hang tight? I won't be long."

She nodded. At least, she thought she nodded. Her heart was pounding so hard, she felt faint. And it wasn't pounding because they'd been caught off guard, either. Oh, no. It was pounding, because she realized she was starting to need this man's touch and his gazes and his words the way she needed food and water and sleep. They breathed life into her.

She watched him jog up the stairs to join Gilberto, ruffling the boy's hair as they walked companionably side by side the rest of the way.

Rousing from his brief nap, Captain lifted his head, looked for his master, and, when he saw that Derek was leaving without him, let out a whimper of protest.

"Yeah, me, too." Willa rubbed his tummy, settling him down so he wouldn't have to tax his elderly joints by getting up to follow. With a sigh, the dog flopped back to the floor, allowing Willa's touch to mollify him.

If only she could be appeased that easily. For her, however, one thing was clear. No man's touch, no man's presence but Derek's was going to suffice. For the first time in forever she knew exactly what she wanted: more. More kisses, more whispers in the night. More of the feeling she had when he looked at her, his eyes heavy with desire.

Lifting Captain's ear, she murmured, "Can you keep a secret? Tonight's the night. I'm going to seduce the sheriff. And defeat is not an option. Okay with you?"

Captain swished his feathery tail. His tongue lolled out of a doggy grin as he panted.

She patted his belly. “Good doggy. I’ll take that as a yes.”

Chapter Eleven

It took Derek longer to put Gilberto to bed than he'd intended. The kid had never had a bedtime routine before, and he loved to review his day—in detail. They were also reading the first *Diary of a Wimpy Kid* together, a very big deal since Gilberto previously thought he hated to read. Being read to for the first time in his life had proved to be the game changer for him, and Derek didn't want to break the spell. Try as he had to shorten their routine tonight, it had still consumed thirty minutes.

He'd come back downstairs concerned that Willa might have gotten bored or annoyed because yet another moment rightfully belonging to her had been handed over to Gilberto. He was being the kind of date most single women he knew would lambaste, unless they were parents. Or wanted to be.

As he reached the living room, he saw Willa curled up on the floor pillows with Captain. She'd tucked an afghan around the old dog, and her hand rested on his side. Silhouetted against the firelight, the curve of her waist and hip made his fingers tingle with the desire to trace them. Her hair glowed with red and gold flames.

He paused on the last step, unsure of his next move, which had happened more since he'd met Willa than at any other time in his life. Knowing what he wanted did not translate easily, however, into knowing how to get it. He'd spent a day and an evening so close to the life he wanted, he could taste it.

When she turned her head and smiled dreamily, he knew he couldn't trust himself to walk over and kiss her; the night would end up very quickly in his bed. And as much as he wanted that, he refused to settle for it. He wouldn't accept anything less than everything she had to give.

So instead of joining her, he walked to the kitchen, grimly holding himself in check and returning a few moments later with a mug of hot cider, which he handed to her.

Resettling herself on the sofa, she accepted the mug, inhaled the aroma of apple and spices, and peeked up at him. "This smells incredible."

"I buy it from Springer Sisters. Have you been out there?" Willa shook her head. "It's an orchard on Highway 35. Four sisters run it. They have a store and a restaurant, too." He gave his stomach a pat. "I ate a lot of their pies before you showed up."

"You wouldn't know it," she complimented, and he felt his ab muscles flex involuntarily.

There was something different in her manner tonight. Her tone bordered on flirtatious. Her gaze was bolder. When she patted the sofa cushion next to her, his self-control became a bad joke.

Taking the mug from her hands, he set it on the table

and cupped the back of her neck, pulling her in for a kiss. Warm and pillow-soft, her lips tasted of apples and cinnamon. When he nudged them apart, she complied eagerly, turning the teasing nibbles into something deeper and more urgent. *Oh, man, the woman knows how to kiss.*

Clinging to Derek's shoulders, Willa pulled back and glanced toward the top of the stairs. "Is Gilberto all settled in?" she asked breathlessly.

"Asleep before I left the room."

Her forehead against Derek's, she nodded slightly. "It's getting late."

His gut clenched as he tried to stem the tide of desire rolling through him. "I didn't expect the night to go so long. I can't leave Gilberto. How am I going to drive you home?"

"Hmm." Brow furrowed in a mock frown, she murmured, "That is a problem. Let me think. I suppose, if necessary, I could stay the night. Just to help you out." Her eyes were large and bright.

"I appreciate that more than I can say." Derek's breath felt labored, and he was sitting still. As far as his libido was concerned, all systems were go. There was a guest bedroom on the first floor, far away from the child sleeping upstairs. Perfect.

As his body prepped for a touchdown dance, however, his brain slapped him upside the head. He'd learned a long time ago that dreams required time and patience, two things in short supply when he wanted Willa with every fiber of his being.

Reaching for her hand, he got to his feet and pulled her with him toward the stairs. He was about to take a calculated risk.

When they reached the second-floor landing, he said, "I always have an extra toothbrush on hand."

"For all your women friends?" she teased.

"I have only one." He planted a swift, hard kiss on her upturned lips.

The flush of pleasure that filled her cheeks made it nearly impossible to do what he knew he had to.

At the end of the hall, two broad double doors led to his master suite. Inviting her into the most intimate space in his home, he watched her reaction. Would she view it the way he had the day the ranch had become his? More than any other room in the house, this one beckoned him to picture a future here with a partner to share it.

Slowly, Willa turned to take in his California king-sized bed and the puffy comforter in an earth-toned Aztec print. The walls were made up of the flat side of split logs, sanded and polished with white chinking in between, giving the room a lodge-resort feel. But his favorite part was the wall of windows facing the now-dark Thunder Ridge range.

"Amazing," Willa murmured.

"I like it a lot. I like it even more with you here."

He wanted her in that king-sized bed, opening her gorgeous stormy eyes to the sight of the mountain. He wanted a love as strong, as permanent as Thunder Ridge itself.

If he and Willa made love tonight, it would be incredible. But dangerous, too, affirming that they were having an affair and suggesting he could be satisfied by the bits and pieces of her life that she was willing to share.

The parameters she'd set for their relationship were built on a foundation of some trauma she refused to confide. Someday, it would be different. He would wait. He would wait as long it took.

"I have a T-shirt you can wear," he told her.

"Will I *need* something to sleep in?"

Time stopped. Their gazes caught and held. Taking a big breath, he tucked her hair behind her ears. "Couple years ago, I came home after a really hard day and made a pan of brownies. I couldn't wait for them to be ready, so I took them out of the oven early. After the first bite, I knew I'd blown it. They were like pudding in the middle. I figured I could put them back in the oven and try again, but they were never right after that, and I realized it was possible to ruin something that should have been great, by trying to hurry it. Know what I mean?"

Willa frowned heavily. "I know you need baking lessons. And this is a really weird time to be talking about brownies."

His laughter was self-deprecating. "Right on both counts. I suck at parables." Holding her face between his hands, he looked into her eyes. "I don't want brownies. I want us. I want us to come out right, Willa. I think that's going to take more time."

Her lips parted. Two spots of color appeared on her cheeks. "But we've known each other over a year."

He could see her confusion. She was trying to process his sudden change in direction. *Damn.* He wanted to kick his own butt for not handling this better. Tamping down his guilt, he crossed to his dresser, withdrew the T-shirt and handed it to her.

"Clean towels are in the master bath and toothbrush is in the medicine cabinet. TV, radio, phone are at your disposal. Use anything you want." Her gaze lowered to the cotton T she held tightly in her hands. "I'll be in the guest room, second door on the left as you enter the hallway, if you need anything. Will you be all right?"

She nodded without looking up.

"Sweet dreams," he said quietly.

He left the room, acutely aware that she hadn't answered.

Two mornings later, the bells on Something Sweet's door jangled, alerting Willa that another customer had arrived. The early birds had already come and gone, and the eight o'clock, post-school drop-off crowd wouldn't swoop in for several more minutes.

Willa nearly dropped an entire tray of onion bialys as Derek filled her doorway. Instantly, her pulse accelerated in anticipation, flagrantly disobeying her brain, which said, *He has a lot of explaining to do.*

Last night, she had slept in her own bed again, though "slept" was a misnomer. Mostly, she had tossed and turned and wrestled with covers that had felt too hot and too heavy even though it was still snowing outside.

She hadn't stopped thinking about Derek for more than a couple of minutes at a time in the past thirty-two hours, having tossed and turned all night at his place, too. For the second time, Derek had primed the pump like a man dying of thirst and then walked away from the well. *What was up with that?* His stories about immediate gratification and undercooked brownies did not cut it as an explanation.

Smiling, he ambled up, resting his arms on the high glass display case. He looked clear-eyed, energetic, fresh as a daisy. *I hate him.* Lack of sleep had drawn dark circles beneath her eyes, and, having spent her mental energy on fretting, she hadn't had the motivation to do anything more this morning than swipe on some lip gloss and sweep her hair into a bun.

"Good morning." His voice reminded her of the coffee she was brewing, smooth and rich.

With Gilberto present the morning after she'd slept at Derek's, Willa hadn't had the opportunity to address her confusion over the way the night had ended. Truthfully, she hadn't even known how to go about it. Now, with him standing right in front of her, she felt heat rise up her neck and into her cheeks. She still had no idea how to ask, *Why don't you want to make love to me?*

Her eyes pricked with tears just from thinking it. Lowering her head, she gave herself a stern talking to while she transferred bialys to the display case. *Keep your cool. Do not hint that you feel rejected. I forbid you to sound pathetic. He's acting like nothing happened, so that is exactly what you'll do.*

"Hi there," she said breezily. "Nice to see you this morning. Would you like some coffee? There's a fresh pot brewing." With rapid movements, she placed the last of the bialys in the case. "Not that you look like you need the caffeine. Uh-uh. You seem very well rested. I'm going to put this tray away and be right back." Baking sheet in hand, she stomped to the kitchen, let the tray clatter into the sink and, ignoring Norman Bluehorse's uncharacteristically inquisitive look, returned to the front.

Back behind the counter, she refused to look Derek in the eye. For the first time, she saw that he'd placed a sheet of neon-yellow paper on the glass top. "What's that?" She pointed.

Glancing down as if he hadn't noticed it, either, he looked so gorgeously masculine and thickheaded, she almost forgave him on the spot.

"It's a flyer. About Rudy Gunnersun's barn dance." He sounded as uncomfortable as she felt. "This Friday."

"I heard about it. Do you want me to put the flyer up in my window?"

His expression said that was the furthest thing from his mind. "No. I came to ask if you'd go with me."

"Oh. I see." She heard her foot tapping the stained-concrete floor. "Actually, no, I don't see." Had he somehow missed the signals she was giving him? "Look, I appreciate the dates, this whole courtship thing, but in case I haven't made myself perfectly clear—I'm easy."

Her heart thumped against her ribs. Well. That was

more forward than she'd been in years. Actually, more forward than she'd ever been.

Derek put his hands on his hips, studying her. "No." He shook his head. "You sure as hell are not."

"Okay, I walked right into that one. I realize I'm not the easiest *person*. We've already covered that territory. But as far as a sexual relationship goes, I invited you back to my house with no time limit on how long you could stay, which I think was a pretty big hint, and the other night, I told you I wanted to spend the night with you at your place."

"You think that makes you a sure bet?"

She gaped at him. "Uh…yeah. Derek, I flat out told you I'm ready for an affair. And you walked away. Twice. What more does a woman need to do to convince you she wants to sleep with you? Put a rose between her teeth and dance naked on the coffee table?"

"Sounds promising," he said drolly. "You said some pretty important things just now. I want to address them. But not here."

"I shouldn't have even brought it up. There are too many ears, and I have too much to do."

"Okay. Tonight then? No, wait—" He frowned. "I have Gilberto now, and I haven't asked anyone yet if they'd be willing to babysit an eleven-year-old boy."

"With an excess of energy," she added.

"Exactly. And I'm not comfortable leaving him on his own yet."

"I'd offer to watch him, of course, but…"

"That would defeat the purpose."

"Right."

"And I want to talk soon. Which brings us back to Friday."

"The barn dance?" she said doubtfully, setting the plates on a serving tray. "Not exactly private."

"Could be. I responded to a suspected prowler call once at Rudy's place. I know all the hideaways. And Gilberto will have other kids to hang with. My guess is we won't have any trouble finding time to talk about...your concerns."

Her biggest concern was that she'd somehow misread him. But he was right: she didn't want to spend any more time obsessing about it, so they needed to talk about it soon.

As the bell on the door jangled again, she said, "The morning rush is about to start. I'd better get to work."

"Okay." Derek cocked his finger at her. "Friday. 'Berto and I will pick you up at six." Leaning close, he murmured, "I'd like to kiss you."

He would? She pulled her lower lip between her teeth to keep from smiling like a ninny. "Oh?"

"Yeah, but that would be like taking out a front-page ad in the *Thunder Ridge Gazette*."

She nodded. "That's probably pushing it."

He reached for her hand and raised it to his lips. Goose bumps shivered along her arm.

Releasing her with a smile, he headed for the door, holding it as moms in sweatpants and heavy boots tumbled in. "Good morning, ladies," he nodded, tossing one final look back at Willa, who stared after him as he walked down the street.

Okay, snap out of it now. Immediately, she started a second pot of coffee, knowing she'd be pouring steadily for the next hour. It was back to business as usual. *Thank heavens.*

Rudy Gunnersun's giant barn was so well lit, Willa could see the glow spilling over the landscape and into the hills.

As she, Derek and Gilberto walked from Derek's truck to the wide-open doors, she spied half the town inside, warmed by a wealth of heat lamps and the music of Hanging by a Thread, an all-female, all-strings band. Entertained by vigorous fiddling, Rudy's guests gathered around food tables set against the far wall under the haymow or lined up in front of kegs that flowed with cider and beer.

Everyone knew the festivities were part of Rudy's bid to oust Thunder Ridge's incumbent mayor, and it wasn't as if Rudy tried to hide that fact. Giant posters with his smiling face decorated every wall.

"Vote FUN, Vote GunnerSUN?" Derek read one of the captions. "It looks like Rudy's running for the mayor of Never-Never Land."

"Shh," Willa chided, trying to stifle a grin. "Do you think Mayor Ellison is concerned about an upset? There are an awful lot of people here."

"Ellison has an indoor softball tournament scheduled for next week. The same people will be there."

The hand Derek placed on the small of her back and the grin he sent her made her feel as if they'd been a couple for years and that this was simply another of those small-town social engagements they were required to keep. It didn't feel bad at all.

"I see my friends," Gilberto told them, waiting for the okay from Derek before running off to hang with them.

Out of uniform tonight, Derek was hands down the best-looking man in the barn. Or in town.

Or possibly in the state, Willa thought as she studied her date. A V-neck knit sweater in a deep wine color topped black jeans that left no doubt about the sheriff's level of fitness. His arms looked as strong as a lumberjack's, and his belly was flat. Over the sweater, he wore a leather jacket as black as his hair.

She had decided to wear heels tonight, hoping to make it easier to dance with a man ten inches taller. Even in her stack-heeled boots, however, he dwarfed her by the sheer breadth of his shoulders and chest. Still, his gaze, his touch, left her feeling strong as well as cherished.

"What are you thinking? Right now," he demanded.

Willa responded immediately with the truth. "That you're not at all my type."

Rearing his head back, Derek released the most robust laugh she'd heard from him yet. She loved that he was so settled in his own skin, so comfortable he didn't offend easily.

"What's your type?" he asked.

She considered. "Refined. Intellectual. More yuppie, less classic macho hero."

The hand on her back began massaging in slow circles. His eyes lowered in heavy-lidded seduction mode. "You had me at 'classic macho hero.'"

It was Willa's turn to laugh, pleasure filling her right down to her toes. She was happy when she was with Derek. Just…happy. "Would you like to dance, Sheriff?"

With the hand that was on her back, he pressed her close. "I sure would. As I recall, dancing together is something you and I do very well. Let's go."

Taking her hand, he led her to the dance floor, where they started out two-stepping to "All About Tonight" and slow danced while Hanging by a Thread played "Bless the Broken Road." The band announced a break, and the couples on the floor began to disperse, all except Willa and Derek, who continued to sway while looking into each other's eyes.

"You wanted an explanation for why we haven't made love yet."

The mere thrum of his voice sent internal shivers racing through her veins. Everywhere they touched, her body felt awake and on fire.

"Now would be a really unfortunate time to mention that you're gay." She spoke hoarsely, relieved when the corners of his eyes crinkled.

"I'm not."

"Whew." She glanced around them at the nearly empty dance floor. "So, it's not exactly private out here. Given the nature of our conversation, I mean."

"Hide in plain sight. Best tactic ever invented."

"If you say so." A devil dancing in his eyes mesmerized her. He could tell her almost anything right now, and she'd believe it.

"I'm not a one-night man," Derek said, his expression and voice turning instantly more serious. "And you are not a one-night woman."

She blinked, genuinely confused. "Who said anything about one night?"

"One night, one week…if you put a time limit on it, it's sex, not a relationship."

"Okay, you kinda sounded like a girl just then."

The cockeyed grin she loved came out in full force. "I may be macho, but I'm also deeply sensitive."

"That time, you managed to sound sexy. Bravo." Facetiously, she asked, "Sooo, you're afraid I'll take you for granted?"

Until that moment, they had continued to sway, even though the music had stopped. Now Derek stilled. "I don't want to take *you* for granted."

This time, emotion caused the shivers that ran through her body, and that was far more dangerous than sexual shivers. "You would never take me for granted," she whispered, knowing it was the absolute truth. "Ever."

Tightening his hold on her waist, he lowered his head.

They stood on the dance floor, forehead to forehead, the sliver of space between them electrified by anticipation. Just a tiny move toward each other, and they'd be kissing. They both knew how good that was.

A bright flash temporarily blinded Willa.

"What do you think you're doing?" Derek's irritated snap surprised Willa almost as much as the flash of light.

"Smile! You two look so cute together. Can I interest you in a souvenir photo? All proceeds go toward the Gunnersun mayoral campaign."

"I don't believe it." Derek rolled his eyes. "Who gave you a camera?"

Holliday Bailey shot Derek her trademark wide, sexy smile. "Rudy. He saw some of my photos in the library. I'm taking a photography class online. It turns out I have a natural gift. Just one among many." She batted her long lashes.

When Willa had first worked at the deli, she'd spent a fair amount of time wondering if the ever-bickering Holliday and Derek were interested in each other. Now she knew the opposite was true: they annoyed the heck out of each other. Sometimes on purpose.

"If this dance had a king and queen, you'd get my vote," Holliday purred then opened her eyes wide. "Hey, what a great idea! We'll start an impromptu ballot. I'm sure I can scrounge up a tiara."

"Don't even think about it." Derek glowered in warning.

The redhead laughed. "Speaking of killjoys, you'd better check on the little man you've been palling around with. He was last seen polishing off the dessert table."

"So that's where he's been." Willa looked at Derek. "He's going to make himself sick. We'd better go."

"How about we let Derek do the dirty work?" Looping her arm through Willa's, Holliday tugged her away. "He's not allowed to keep you all to himself now that you're finally out of the bakery. We girls can grab something to eat with Izzy and a few members of the Thursday night book club. I know they'd love for you to recommend your favorite cookbooks."

Holliday kept chatting while Willa tried not to look back at Derek for rescue, or to think about the almost-kiss Holliday had interrupted. She spent the next quarter hour or so chatting with Izzy and with Holliday's book group, which included Carly Levine, Gilberto's fifth-grade teacher.

"It's amazing, the progress Gilberto has made since he moved in with Sheriff Neel." Carly, who, Willa guessed, was in her thirties, beamed. "And the tutoring you've been giving him has been seriously helpful, Willa. He talks about it. His self-esteem has skyrocketed, and his attendance has jumped from forty to one hundred percent. Everyone at school is thrilled. Thank you."

"Don't thank me," Willa demurred. "Derek's the one holding the reins. I think Gilberto is his special project."

"That's great, but don't sell yourself short," Carly said. "If he's ever had a woman in his life before, this is the first time it's shown." She looked around the room. "I'd better go find my husband. I've left him alone far too long to talk local politics with city council members. Makes him cranky."

After Carly left, Izzy said, "She's right. You're both doing a great job with that boy."

"Well, Derek is doing the lion's share. I'm only helping out." Her gaze swept the room, lighting on Derek and Gilberto next to one of the dessert tables, deep in conversation with Izzy's husband, Nate, and their son, Eli. As she and Izzy watched the foursome, Derek said something that made Eli laugh and sock him on the shoulder. Gilberto guffawed so hard, he doubled over. "He really is a natural with kids," Willa murmured.

Izzy grinned fondly. "Always has been."

When she'd first worked at the deli, Willa had been struck by the extent of Derek's involvement in Eli's life. A single mother until recently, Izzy's situation apparently had been complicated by a lack of education and a family to whom she could turn for help. On top of that, Eli had been severely hearing impaired since age two. As Izzy's best friend, Derek had learned American Sign Language to communicate with Eli and had been the central male figure in the young man's life until Nate returned and began to build a relationship with his son.

"I don't know if you remember," Izzy said, watching her men, "but Derek tangled with Nate when they first met."

"I do remember."

"Derek was the main man in Eli's life for so long. He had to slide over to make room for Nate. It was difficult."

Oh, my gosh. How dumb am I? Willa thought abruptly. Taking care of Gilberto represented a whole lot more than an act of extreme volunteerism. In a very real sense, Derek had lost his "family" when Nate arrived on the scene. Taking care of Gilberto filled a big, big hole.

"He's wanted a family of his own for a long time," Izzy confirmed. "Is that what you want?"

She said it kindly enough, but her concern was evident.

"Derek knows where I stand," Willa said carefully. "I've been clear." But then Derek's words leaped to mind. *If you put a time limit on it, it's sex, not a relationship.* "And, of course, we're still talking about it," she stumbled as worry niggled at the back of her mind. But he *did* know where she stood, didn't he?

Izzy stared at her a moment longer, then nodded. "Have you tried the pear and gorgonzola crostini?" She reached for one of the hors d'oeuvres on the table beside them and took a bite. "Delicious. You think a pear-gorgonzola knish would fly at the deli?"

With the subject changed, they spent the next few minutes discussing new recipes Izzy wanted to introduce at The Pickle Jar. Willa's attention, however, never strayed from the man they both cared about so deeply.

Chapter Twelve

Once the applause died down and the lights in the Thunder Ridge Elementary School gymnasium buzzed back on, Willa allowed herself to exhale. The fifth-grade history pageant was now history itself, and Gilberto had rocked the part of Daniel Boone. She and Derek had been clutching each other's hands since Gilberto's first appearance onstage.

"I think I'd have been calmer during a high-speed chase," Derek said, looking quite adorably serious about that.

Willa laughed. "It might have been less nerve-racking if we'd had more notice he was going to be Daniel Boone. Under the circumstances, I think a little anxiety is justified."

Originally cast in a less pivotal role, Gilberto stepped up to fill Daniel Boone's moccasins when the boy previously set to play the part announced that his family had sold their home and was moving. Willa was sure Carly

Levine had transferred the role to Gilberto to boost his self-esteem now that she knew there were adults who could be counted on to help. Although the teacher had assured Derek that Gilberto could carry the script if he needed to, the eleven-year-old had refused even to consider that option. Offered his first chance to shine in school, he'd been determined to give it all he had.

Derek squeezed Willa's hand. "If it wasn't for you, the kid would have had to wear a cardboard sign that said 'I am Daniel Boone' as a costume. Thank you for not complaining that every would-be date seems to turn into a family affair. The next date is ours alone. You have my word." He rubbed the back of her neck and the spot right below her ear. "Have I told you how grateful I am that you've been by my side through this?"

"One hundred and forty-two times in the past ten days alone. This makes a hundred and forty-three."

Shaking his head regretfully, he murmured in that resonant baritone, "I should have done it more."

How did he make the most innocuous statement sound like verbal foreplay? "I enjoyed it," she murmured back, and she really had. Gilberto's enthusiasm was always infectious, and Derek's fumbling attempts to sew had been flat-out endearing. Willa had wound up making Gilberto a Daniel Boone costume with a fringed jacket and faux coonskin cap. And, when she wasn't sewing or helping him draft his speech, she and Gilberto had hiked one of her favorite sections of Long River to gather props and get into character.

If she and Derek hadn't found the time to resume the discussion about whether they were going to have an "affair" or a "relationship," well, that was a bonus as far as she was concerned. Everything was so good right now, so easy and natural. Couldn't they just enjoy it awhile?

"I don't think he took his eyes off you during his entire speech," Derek commented.

"Because he was afraid of forgetting his lines." Willa laughed. "Daniel Boone was supposed to have said, 'I have never been lost, but I will admit to being confused for several weeks.' Not the other way around."

"I wondered about that." Derek chuckled. "Come on. Let's find Mr. Boone before he's mobbed by fans."

His proud smile tugged at her heart.

"Sounds good."

As they blended into the line of parents and other family members snaking into the hallway, he brushed a light kiss at her temple.

She inhaled sharply. Sometimes she got swept up in the idea that she wanted this to last. As the throng milled around them, pressing them toward the PTA's snack tables, Willa tried to focus on the smell of hot coffee, the freshly popped corn—anything but the temptation to stay where she was, right here with Derek and Gilberto, finding her place in life again by loving a man and a child.

They inched forward, and her gaze roved the art projects that covered the hall walls. Did one of these drawings belong to Gilberto? Did anyone care? She did, she realized, as children pushed through the crowd to reach their parents. She cared very much.

"How'd I do?"

It took a moment for Willa to realize Gilberto had squeezed between her and Derek and was peering eagerly into their faces.

"My man, Daniel Boone! Is it really you?" Derek leaned far forward, pretending to scrutinize Gilberto's face and the faux fur hat. "You were amazing up there, Dan. Can I have your autograph?"

"Cut it out," Gilberto complained, looking around to

see if anyone was listening, but his grin conveyed more pride than embarrassment. "What did you think, Willa?"

He looked so earnest, so desiring of her approval. Memory pinched her heart. *Ignore it. This is a different time, different place. Different people. It's nowhere near the same.* "You were great." Bending close to Gilberto's ear, she said, "The audience loved you. Your research paid off, buddy. Everyone totally believed you were Daniel Boone."

"You really think so?"

"I sure do." It was so easy to fill Gilberto's tank. Her compliments had him beaming.

"There's the man of the hour!" Izzy approached from inside the auditorium to give Gilberto a hug and add her praise to Willa and Derek's.

"You came to see me in the play?" Gilberto asked Izzy in wonder.

"Wouldn't have missed it." She handed him a paper bag tied with a ribbon. "I brought the cream soda you like from the deli. Opening night gift."

"Wow! Thanks. I'm opening it now." Catching himself, he looked up at Derek. "I mean, *may* I drink it now?"

Derek nodded. "Sure. Knock yourself out."

"Can I go find Tyler and share the soda with him?"

"You bet." Derek turned to Izzy as Gilberto trotted off. "Where's Nate?"

"Stacking chairs in the auditorium. Wanna help?"

Tucked into his back pocket, Derek's phone vibrated. He pulled it out and checked the screen. "Sorry, Izz, gotta take this." Kissing Willa on the cheek, he said, "Back in a minute."

"Pretty cute," Izzy commented, taking a few steps forward alongside Willa in the coffee line.

Willa nodded. "He looked adorable in that 'coonskin cap,' didn't he?"

"I meant the three of you."

Oh. Heat suffused Willa's cheeks. Their conversation at the barn dance loomed crystal clear in her mind even though neither woman had referred to it since. Over the past two weeks, Willa had watched Derek in full fatherhood mode and could honestly say he was one of the best men she'd ever known, devoted to his work when he was at work, but equally committed to Gilberto—and to her—when they were together.

Gilberto wasn't the only one blooming in Derek's care.

Emotion welled rapidly, closing off her throat. Feeling foolish, she blinked away the burning sensation in her eyes.

"Hey." Concerned, Izzy tugged Willa out of line. "Everything all right?"

Intending to deny there was a problem, Willa instead heard herself exclaim, "I don't want to hurt him." And then she was crying. *Oh, for pity's sake.* Had she held on to her precious control for all this time only to let go now?

Izzy spoke quietly. "I'm assuming that by 'him,' you're referring to Derek." She dug into her purse for a tissue and handed it to Willa, who accepted gratefully.

"Yes. Derek."

"Then come clean with him."

Willa froze mid nose blow. She'd never discussed her past with Izzy. "What…what do you mean?"

"Whatever is bothering you—*whatever it is*—Derek can handle it. Truly. He has very broad shoulders." For the first time in their acquaintance, Izzy put her arms around Willa, giving her a reassuring hug. "I know how hard it is to trust yourself with his heart. But it really will be okay."

"I—I know," Willa whispered, but she didn't. Not really. Izzy had hit the nail on the head. Could she count on herself to take care of Derek's heart? If they were ever going to move forward, she had no choice. A voice inside her head said loudly, *He deserves the truth.*

As they arrived at the head of the concession line, Derek reappeared, looking shell-shocked.

Willa handed him a coffee. "You look like you could use something stronger," she said. "What's wrong?"

Accepting the cup, he nodded toward the quiet hallway where he'd taken the call. "Let's talk over there. Is 'Berto still off with his friend?"

"Yes." Willa traded a concerned glance with Izzy.

"The call was from Jeanne," Derek said when they reached a relatively private spot, "Gilberto's social worker. She phoned to tell me Roddy's gone."

"Gone?" Willa shook her head. "Where?"

"No one knows. According to his roommates, he packed up all his things along with plenty of theirs and split. No forwarding address. They want to press charges for theft." Derek's eyes flashed lightning. "He's completely abandoned Gilberto."

Unmindful of Izzy or anyone else who might be watching, Willa wrapped Derek in a hug. She felt his strong body relax into her embrace as he allowed her to comfort him. "What happens now?" she asked.

Derek pulled back enough to be heard by both women, but kept an arm firmly around Willa. "According to Jeanne, this wasn't the first time Roddy was caught giving alcohol to minors. He's permanently off the list of potential providers for Gilberto, and there are no other family connections suitable or interested in providing care at this point."

"That stinks," Izzy exclaimed, her own background no doubt adding fuel to the fire in her tone. "Gilberto is at the mercy of people who can't get their acts together?"

"Not necessarily." Derek looked into Willa's eyes.

"Jeanne asked if I'd be on board for long-term foster care." He paused. "Or permanent guardianship."

"Are you?" Izzy asked.

Willa knew the answer before he gave it.

"Yes." He was still looking directly at her, searching for her reaction.

The truth was she'd have been disappointed if he'd made a different decision, because this one was pure Derek. He was a man who stepped up to the plate every time.

She smiled and nodded to offer her support. Even as she did so, however, worry gnawed at her. This complicated things. He needed people who would stick with him and stick around, no matter what challenges came his way.

Now, she realized, they had even more to talk about on Friday—the night they planned, at last, to have a real date, only the two of them. Derek had found an adult eager to hang out with Gilberto for the evening, so they were all set. Willa knew she'd have to do a lot of thinking between now and Friday night. One thing was certain, however. It was time to tell Derek everything.

The week flew by. Even the weather had changed significantly enough to turn the previous days into a distant memory. It had stopped snowing, and though the cold front continued, the streets were clear. By Friday, Willa still hadn't decided exactly how she was going to broach the topic of her past with Derek. The past that, no matter how she tried to deny it, still affected every nook and cranny of her present. Burning off nervous energy, she tidied her house from top to bottom in preparation for his arrival.

The bungalow looked good. Flickering candles emitted a subtle spicy fragrance, and light jazz played in the background. The lamps were on dimmers, and the fireplace was ready for the strike of a match. She had an elegant Hudson

Vineyard Syrah and her grandmother's wine goblets poised on the table. She still needed to put the flowers into vases.

In the kitchen, a sage-and-thyme-crusted prime rib filled the house with its succulent aroma, and her Yorkshire pudding waited patiently to be put in the oven, where it would puff to golden perfection. Lord-of-the-manor food. I-care-about-you-and-want-you-to-feel-special food. Her signature bourbon-spiked creamed spinach still needed to be prepped, but that wouldn't take long, and first she wanted to double-check her bedroom.

From the doorway, she scanned the area, trying to see it through Derek's eyes. What about candles in here? Should she light them now or wait until he arrived? Moving to her bed, she smoothed her hands over the comforter. Fresh sheets? Check. Pillows plumped? Check.

Sexy lingerie? Check.

She fingered the lace peignoir and satin robe she'd laid out. She'd bought the sexy duo only yesterday. The nightie with its plunging neckline and see-through skirt had looked so glamorous, so confidence-inducing in the shop window. Suddenly, though, it seemed dangerously scanty. Playing the seductress had never been her MO, yet tonight she wanted to try it, and she wanted to do it *before* she told Derek about her past life.

Because it's easier to bare your body than your soul.

Sharing her history with him signaled not only the beginning of a new phase in their relationship, it signaled the end of something, too. Up to now, her grief had been private, fierce yet somehow delicate, like a butterfly she had to shield to keep alive. Because keeping the grief alive kept the people for whom she grieved alive. That's how it felt, anyway. If she wanted Derek, she was going to have to slacken her hold on the past. Allow others to disturb her status quo.

A quick glance at the clock told her Derek would be there in just over an hour. Her stomach felt like a crazy soup of foreboding and anticipation and yearning. She didn't even bother to convince herself she was ready for this moment; she knew only that she wanted it. *Seduce first, talk second. Everything will be okay.*

And then the doorbell rang.

What?

Derek had said he'd arrive at eight. It was only seven.

Willa's pulse leaped wildly. Dinner wasn't ready, and she still hadn't decided for sure about the negligee.

"Just a minute!" she called then glanced at the mirror, flustered. *Crumbs*, she hadn't even had time to do her hair and makeup. Derek was always punctual, sometimes early—and he had called twice today, saying he couldn't wait for this evening—but an *hour* early? For a date? No fair.

As suddenly as it arrived, though, her panic subsided. She'd wanted to be naked at some point on this date. Might as well start with a naked face. Apparently, she wasn't meant to hide behind anything tonight.

Taking a deep breath, she headed for the front door.

Although she hadn't yet turned on the porch light, through the leaded glass panes, Willa could see the shadow of a man. As she unlocked the deadbolt, she teased, "You must be as excited about tonight as I—"

Her voice faltered.

Time and her pulse both seemed to stop as she realized that the person on her porch was not Derek.

"Jase?" she whispered. Or thought she'd whispered. Had a sound actually emerged?

It's an illusion. Your mind is playing tricks.

But he smiled, and it was the smile she remembered,

the one that had once made her feel all was right with the world.

She raised a trembling hand to her lips. The blue eyes she knew so well filled with too many emotions to count… apprehension, guilt, gratitude…

"Hello, Willa," he said raggedly. "I'm back."

Chapter Thirteen

The man Willa had married when she was still just a girl reached out and hugged her tightly, almost uncomfortably so, but she understood the impulse. It was nearly impossible to believe he was here, that he was alive at all after so much time without a single bit of contact. The emotion she'd staved off for two years broke loose, bit by bit, like stones tumbling from a cliff in the moments before an avalanche, and she felt her arms wrap around him, holding him. Her crying left wet patches on the front of his shirt, and she could feel his own tears dampen her neck as he pressed his face into the crook of her shoulder.

She curled her right hand into a fist and thumped it against his chest. "Dammit, Jase. I thought you were dead." His shirt muffled the last, sobbed, word.

"I'm sorry. I'm so sorry."

They stood for a long moment, he just outside her front door and she on the threshold. They clung to each other, attempting to pull themselves together. Finally, Willa leaned back to peer at him through the blur of her tears.

He was leaner now. Almost hollow. His clothes were far more casual than the designer shirts and suits he'd once favored, their starched-and-pressed perfection gone entirely. The Jase she remembered could have stepped out of a menswear catalogue. The man in front of her looked disheveled.

"Any chance you'll let me in?" he asked, uncharacteristic hesitation shadowing his words.

A tiny hiccup escaped her. "Of course." She stood back and held the door wide. "Please."

Jase stepped past her into the cozy cottage she'd so carefully set for seduction and glanced around with abject curiosity. "You…uh—" he cleared his throat, running a hand over his stubbled jaw "—expecting someone?"

"Yes." The blood surged hotly to her cheeks as she nudged the door shut with her hip. "But not for an hour. Sit down." She gestured to the sofa.

Awkwardly, he nodded, sitting on the edge of a cushion as if he couldn't quite commit.

"This is a nice place," he said.

She shrugged. The house they'd shared in California, a remodeled Mediterranean that he, especially, had loved, had been four times the size of this one. "It's small. But I like it. It's home now," she acknowledged simply.

He nodded. Long fingers, perfect for a surgeon, curled over his knees. "I rehearsed what I was going to say. You know? And now here I am, and…" He shrugged, getting to his feet, his body a bundle of nervous energy that refused to let him settle. Willa watched him cross to the fireplace as if he knew exactly what he'd find there.

Slowly raising a hand, he touched the framed photo she'd kept in her bedroom the past several weeks. Tonight she had brought it into the living room again, because she wanted Derek to see it.

"This is the only photo I took with me when I left," Jase commented. "It's my favorite."

Willa felt the muscles in her stomach clench. She forced herself to inhale. "Mine, too."

The picture showed their daughter, Sydney, at age ten, in a photo snapped right before her fifth-grade spring dance.

"Everything made sense before she died. Nothing made sense after," Jase said roughly. "I honest-to-God don't know how you went through it stone-cold sober, Will. You were the strong one."

Willa's body gave a little jerk while her mind tried to process that. Did simply surviving mean she was strong? Hiding in a new town, in a tiny bungalow meant for her alone, sidestepping human entanglements? She hadn't felt strong at all. After their beautiful Sydney died, the world turned upside down and stayed there, until just recently.

She looked at her candles, smelled the prime rib still cooking, remembered the nightie. Unbidden, anger joined the myriad other emotions rocking around her body. For so long, she'd dreamed of the moment he would show up unexpectedly, and she would realize he was still alive. But that moment hadn't come. Now, without a call, without the merest hint of warning, he was here.

"Where the hell have you been, Jason? It's been two years of pure torture. I thought you were dead. We all did. You sent me divorce papers and a note that told me basically nothing except that you couldn't handle our marriage anymore. You haven't even contacted your *parents* in all this time. After losing a child yourself, how could you—" She slapped her hands over her mouth. She'd relegated rage to the back of the line behind worry and grief. Now it was front and center, poised to launch an arrow straight into Jase's heart for leaving her to handle so much on her own and for making them all grieve twice.

"Go on," he said when she stopped. "Whatever you have to say, I deserve it. And I've probably already said it to myself." He returned Sydney's picture carefully to the mantel and faced his ex-wife. "I was a fraud, Willa. I loved medicine, but I worshipped the idea that I could fix whatever was broken, and when I couldn't help our own daughter—" He blew a frustrated sigh at the ceiling. "The guilt drove me to my knees. I damn near—" Raw emotion twisted his features. "I didn't think I was going to make it. Leaving everyone seemed like the right thing. I'm not saying it was, only that my mind made it seem that way. I'll never be able to tell you how sorry I am for putting you through everything I did. I don't expect you to give me your forgiveness. I just need you to know that I'm asking."

Outside, a dog barked. A siren rose then faded into the distance and a car whooshed down the street, too fast. Life in Thunder Ridge carried on, oblivious to their struggle.

There were so many questions, but Willa knew the most important ones couldn't be answered. Not in this lifetime. They would never understand why they had been so lucky, so blessed with the magic that had been their family. Or why it had all had to end.

Jase managed a wobbly smile. "Thanks for keeping my lawyer in the loop about where you're living."

Wordlessly, she nodded.

He glanced around again. "You're building a life for yourself here."

"Trying to."

"I'm proud of you, Will. You're a survivor."

Silent tears slipped down her cheeks. He had come to give her the gift of closure on a marriage that had taken her from girl to wife to mother. He'd given her Syd, and the truth was that as long as she lived she would be Syd's mother, her favorite role of all. In return, Willa could give Jase the one thing he couldn't give himself.

"You're forgiven," she whispered. "Believe it, Jase. You're forgiven." She wasn't sure who made the first move, but suddenly they were in each other's embrace for one final hug.

The familiar arms tightened briefly before he leaned back to look at her. "How long did it take you to believe you really could move forward?"

"I think…it took until just now."

They shared a long moment of understanding neither would ever have with anyone else. The doorbell jarred them both.

Through the picture window to the right of her front door, Willa saw Derek, standing close to the glass. Close enough for her to see that he wasn't merely standing on the porch; he was staring into the house at her and Jase.

It didn't take long for her to react. She left Jase's arms immediately and ran to the door, flinging it open. "Derek! Come in."

A burst of cold air entered with him. Willa felt so overheated, she welcomed it.

"I'm glad you're here," she said, the words rushing out. This was so *not* how she wanted him to find out about her life as a wife and mother. Her mind raced as she tried to figure out what he was thinking.

"I'm early." Voice and expression grim, he stared at Jase as he asked Willa, "Bad timing?"

"No," she lied and gestured to Jase. "We were…" *Oh, boy. What?*

Derek looked at her. His shoulders squared, his brow lowered, he had an *I-could–kick-this-guy's-ass-easily* look on his face. Yet, underneath, she saw an uncertainty that made her want to kiss him until he looked like Derek again.

"I get the feeling I'm interrupting," Derek deadpanned.

"No. I am." Stepping forward, Jase extended a hand. "Hi. I'm Jason Holmes. And you are?"

"Derek Neel. Sheriff of Thunder Ridge." Warily, he reached for the outstretched hand, his expression puzzling out the connection. "Holmes? You're related to Willa?"

"In a manner of speaking. I married her about fourteen years ago, just out of high school."

Derek went pale. A long, awkward moment of silence followed before he found his voice. "In that case, I suppose you two have a lot of catching up to do. I'll leave you to it." Turning, he strode through the still-open door.

"Derek," Willa called, gripping the doorknob, "don't go."

He crossed the porch and headed down the steps toward his truck.

"Derek, you don't understand." Willa ran after him. His driver's side door slammed. "Please wait!" But he couldn't hear her over the roar of the engine or the angry squeal of tires as he drove away.

It took every ounce of strength, emotional and physical, for Derek to walk calmly into his house, excuse the sitter on the pretext that his stomach was acting up, and spend the rest of the evening watching dumb movies with Gilberto. Every time the phone rang, Derek ignored it, grumbling about telemarketers until he eventually just yanked his landline from the jack and put his cell on "vibrate only" to stave off Gilberto's innocent questions.

Willa had called at least six times, but he was in no mood to talk to anyone, especially not to her, not yet.

Gilberto seemed to sense that he was struggling and

actually went into the kitchen on his own to make Derek a cup of tea laced generously with honey. Then he made sure the throws were tucked in around Derek's legs. The boy's clumsy, well-meaning ministering was the only thing that kept Derek from tearing his house apart, stud by stud.

Once Gilberto found the antacid bottle in the medicine cabinet and offered "something for your sick tummy," he burrowed in next to Derek, peering up every so often with such tender adoration that Derek could barely swallow around the lump in his throat. The kid was so sweet, looking at him as if he hung the moon, when in reality, Derek felt his world crumbling around him.

She was *married*. Married to her high school sweetheart, yet hadn't considered that important enough to tell him. What a fool he'd been. After all the opportunities he'd given her to tell him the truth about her mysterious past, she had a damned husband. One to whom she was obviously still pretty close.

And here he was, the complete dumbass, showing up at her front door, thinking forever was in the cards.

Blood surged through his body like molten lava. Muscles tensed, fists clenched, he muttered an expletive under his breath. Gilberto squirmed around under his blanket and peered at Derek curiously.

"Do you need to throw up? Cuz, if you do, I can go get you a bowl." He looked worried.

Derek inhaled deeply and made a concerted effort to reassure the child at his side. "No, little buddy, I think I just had some heartburn. It's going to be fine, and you know why?"

Gilberto shrugged. "No."

Derek looped an arm around the child's shoulders and pulled him close. "Because you are the best doctor in the whole world. That tea you made me? Has me feeling almost a hundred percent. I'm telling you the truth. I don't know what I'd do without you here to help me through this rough patch."

Gilberto puffed like a peacock. He nodded manfully. "'Kay. I think you probably should go to bed now. I can tuck you in." He looked at the clock and calculated. "It's already past ten, so I'll turn off the TV and let Captain out. You go upstairs, put on your pajamas and brush your teeth, and I'll be up there to say a prayer and stuff, okay?"

Derek pulled the kid up against his chest and ruffled his hair. If Willa had sent fissures splintering through his heart, Gilberto was the sealant that kept it from breaking altogether. "You're the best, buddy. I'll meet you upstairs after you take care of things down here."

Thrilled at the opportunity to play master of the house, Gilberto completed his chores and met Derek, who had watched everything from the top of the stairs.

"You know, because of your help tonight, I feel good enough to tuck you in, dude," Derek said. "I think you totally cured me."

"Yeah, well, I've been thinking 'bout being a doctor."

"No kidding? I always hoped I'd have a doctor in my family." He'd already told 'Berto about Roddy leaving, letting the confusion and grief and anger sit for a day or two before mentioning that Jeanne was trying to find someone who could keep Gilberto safe and take care of him until he was an adult. Then Derek had shared that he'd told Jeanne *he* wanted to be that someone.

Now, as Gilberto heard Derek say the word "family" in relation to them, his mouth dropped open before he snapped it shut and acted too cool for his shoes. He turned away, but not before Derek caught the beginnings of an enormous grin. Another crack in Derek's heart filled as he followed the boy to his room. They were almost through their good-night routine when Captain began to bark incessantly.

Gilberto sat up in bed. "Captain hears something."

Derek had heard a car a couple minutes earlier when Gilberto was starting to nod off during their book time. "Probably some pest getting into the garbage out there. You go to sleep, and I'll take a peek outside, okay?" he said, though he was pretty sure it was Willa.

'Berto nodded and yawned, scooting back down in the bed and rolling onto his side. "If it's a burglar, call me and I'll come and kick him in the yayas for you, okay?"

"Will do." Derek had never had a deputy offer to kick anyone in the yayas for him. He gave the boy a fist bump and left the room telling himself that he and the kid would be fine, just fine on their own. If Willa was outside? She could stay there. He was in no mood to hear an explanation now.

A soft but insistent knocking had Captain doing his ancient best to guard the fortress from attack. Unfortunately, the rusty barking and doused porch light failed to sway Willa, who continued to knock in a restrained way Derek knew was intended not to disturb Gilberto. Hovering at the top of the stairs, he watched her move to the plate glass window. She cupped her hands on the glass, trying to catch a glimpse of life.

He stood silently, willing her to go.

"Derek, I know you're there. Please open up." There was a slight pause. "It's freezing out here." She knocked again. Harder.

He wavered. Just a little.

"Derek?" Gilberto's voice, sleepy yet filled with worry, called out from the bedroom. "I think Willa is here."

Derek sighed in heavy frustration. "I'm on my way down to talk to her. You go to sleep, okay?"

"Okay." Gilberto sounded hesitant. "Good night."

"'Night, partner."

Captain was working himself into an early grave, clawing at the door and whining now that he realized who was there. Using the need to save his dog as an excuse, Derek pushed himself off the top step and walked heavily down the stairs. Flipping on the porch light, he opened the door. Willa huddled inside her coat and rubbed her ungloved hands together. Instantly, he wanted to haul her into his arms and warm her.

Sucker.

Steeling himself, he said, "Willa, go home. I don't feel like talking."

"Derek, hear me out. That's all I'm asking. I was going to tell you everything tonight, but Jase… He showed up and beat me to it."

Her auburn hair was loose, the way he liked it most, cascading in angel-soft waves around her face and her shoulders. Her features looked strained and tense, and her splotchy cheeks told him she'd been crying. His jaws clenched tighter than a vise.

"It's freezing out here," she reiterated. "Let me come in for a few minutes to explain. Please."

He hesitated, and her face filled with uncertainty.

I don't care.

But he did and damned himself for it.

They hovered on the threshold until finally he took a step back. She walked past him.

Shutting the door, he fumbled with a lamp that sent a yellow glow throughout the room.

"Sit." He gestured to a chair in the living room and moved to stoke the fire that he and Gilberto had let die. Shyly, she moved to the chair nearest the hearth and sat, shivering.

"You should have worn mittens."

"I ran out of the house too quickly." Her teeth chattered. "I left right after Jase did."

Jase. "I'm going to get a cup of tea. Want anything?"

"No. I'm good. Thank you."

"Okay. Tea it is." Abruptly, he turned and strode to the kitchen.

No matter what she said, no matter her reason for refusing to share with him a fraction of what she had obviously shared with *Jase*, he wasn't going to give in to his heart, which was once again telling him to let it go, to listen, to love her. His heart was such a dumbass. Well, he was all through letting himself get whomped in the gut. If the question was, "When are you going to learn your lesson?" the answer was, "Right now."

Willa knew Derek could tell she was freezing. Even though she'd caused him great pain, he was still worried about her.

She leaned forward on the sofa, her chilly palms pressed together and tucked between her knees. As he clattered around in the kitchen, she tried to remember everything she needed to tell him tonight, so she could get it all out before he tossed her on her ear. She wouldn't blame him if he did. What he'd walked in on tonight would have thrown anyone for a loop.

After five of the longest minutes in Willa's life, Derek returned with two steaming mugs of tea, their bags bobbing in the water. He pressed one mug into her hands then sat in the recliner across from her. *Fair enough.* An involuntary shiver racked her entire body, and she sloshed her tea. Derek stood, dropped a throw in her lap then returned to his own chair.

"Okay." His sigh was filled with a mix of impatience and resistance. "What do you need to tell me?"

"Everything. From the beginning. Which is what I'd planned to do tonight, before Jase showed up. His arrival was totally unexpected."

"Is that so?"

She didn't know what he disbelieved—that she'd been planning to tell him about her past or that Jase's appearance had come as complete surprise, but the answer to both was, "Yes."

With a steady, uncompromising stare, he said nothing more, merely waited for her to begin. So she did, however awkwardly.

"Jase... Jason Holmes...was my husband. *Was*, being the operative word. Our divorce was final about a year ago, although the marriage ended before that. Before tonight, I hadn't seen Jase in over two years, right before he served the divorce papers."

"He served you?"

"Yes. We'd gone through a rough time. He'd started drinking and taking prescription medication. I wasn't really myself at that point, either, and, well, since I didn't want to kick him while he was down, he went ahead and filed for the divorce himself. Then he disappeared. No one, not even his parents or sister heard from him. To be honest, until I saw his face this evening, I thought he might be dead."

Derek's brows shot up, and she could tell she had his attention. "Why would you think that?"

Willa kept her hands cupped around the hot mug. She took a sip of tea, willing its warmth to penetrate the places inside her that were filled with icy fear.

"Let me back up," she said, "so it'll be easier to understand. Jase was a very gifted surgeon. Pediatrics. We got pregnant when I was twenty. Sydney was a surprise. At first we sort of freaked out, but she was a golden child from the very beginning—happy, funny, healthy and a great sleeper. You can't complain about that, even if the timing isn't what you expected."

Derek set his mug down, his attention riveted, his brow lowered.

"We had help from very doting grandparents. Jase went to medical school and on to his residency, and eventually I went to culinary school. Life was hectic and intense and wonderful. I was happier than I'd ever been. We were all happy."

Derek's jaw worked over that bit of information, but the time for sparing feelings, his or her own, had come to an end. He needed to understand and that meant she had to tell the truth. "You know," she confessed softly, "as much as I loved my culinary career, being Sydney's mom was far and away the best part of me. Nobody could make me laugh like Syd. She practiced jokes before she went to sleep at night."

Willa watched Captain slowly clump around the coffee table, making his way toward her. Ever-so-gently, he laid his graying head in her lap. If she didn't know better, she'd say she saw compassion in his old eyes.

Upstairs, the floor creaked. Gilberto heading to the bathroom, she assumed.

"Oh, I brought a picture to show you." Reaching for her purse, she pulled out the framed 8x10 from her mantel and handed it to him.

Derek studied the photo. "She's the spitting image of you. Beautiful. Really. Beautiful."

Willa smiled. "She was way prettier. Her features were bolder. *She* was bolder. That was taken before her first formal school dance. We went shopping for a dress and spent hours getting her ready."

She watched him read the note and signature slashed across the bottom of the 8x10. *To Mom, From Syd. I love it when you do my hair.*

"She gave me the photo on Mother's Day," Willa said. "That weekend, we were all invited to go on a vacation out at Big Bear Lake with a couple of Syd's friends and their families. Jase was working at Los Angeles Children's Hospital, and I was an executive pastry chef in South Pasadena. He didn't have any surgeries scheduled, but there was no way I could go. Mother's Day weekend is one of the busiest in the food industry. I didn't want them to miss out since I had to work anyway, so I insisted they go without me. Syd gave me my present before they left."

"How old was she in this photo?" Derek asked.

"Almost eleven."

"Same age as Gilberto," he murmured.

"Yes."

"Tell me more about her."

The guarded look that had been on his face since he'd opened the door gave way to an expression of intense listening. Willa took a ragged inhalation. "Syd was a big heart with arms and legs. She never had a 'best' friend, because she loved everyone and assumed they loved her back. Her room was always a mess. She was crazy good at most sports. Swam like a fish. Nothing scared her. Not even the things that should have."

With shaky hands, she raised the mug of tea to her lips and took a long swallow before continuing. "On that Mother's Day weekend, Syd, Jase and a couple other families and their kids camped by the lake near a popular swimming and diving area. From what I was able to gather, Syd watched someone do a backflip off the rocks and decided she wanted to try it. Jase had seen some pretty serious injuries from that kind of thing, and he told her no. I guess when he and the other dads went to turn on the propane tanks in the motorhomes, Sydney climbed up the rocks. She told her friends she wanted to see how high it was. No one knows whether she'd decided to dive despite her father's warning or whether she lost her footing and fell."

Derek's own tea sat untouched on the coffee table now, and he was as still as stone.

"Syd didn't surface. The kids started screaming. One of the mothers searched for her while the other ran for Jase. By the time he reached Sydney, she was out of the water, but unconscious. And by the time Life Flight got her to the hospital and I arrived, she was on life support."

Willa tried to tell the story as a series of facts, but each word that fell from her lips felt like a self-inflicted blow, and she rounded her torso over her legs in a kind of upright fetal position, as if she could protect herself.

"While I stayed with Syd round the clock, Jase called in every favor from every expert he'd ever consulted with and then some, searching for a miracle. He wouldn't leave his office for days at a time. And I sat alone in Syd's room, searching for her in the hospital bed."

Once more, Willa saw the clinic-green walls with their outrageously cheerful decals and the tubes and wires and brilliant, heartbreaking machines that sustained her daughter's breathing.

She closed her eyes. "I thought if I believed hard enough, she would wake up. Be my Syd again." Opening her eyes, she sought Derek's face, willing him to understand. "The moment you stop fooling yourself is the worst moment of all."

"You weren't fooling yourself," Derek responded roughly. "You were hoping. Hope is never wasted."

"Thank you." She wondered if Derek realized he was massaging her back? She didn't want him to stop.

"Where was Jase in all this?" he asked.

"Still wrestling with his own demons. We'd begun to visit Sydney separately. We were arguing horribly, saying things to each other we wouldn't have been able to imagine before the accident."

"What did you argue about?"

"Jase refused what his education told him it was time to admit. That our daughter was gone. And I began to think we'd go crazy if we didn't admit it. I knew I would never, ever, ever understand, but it was time." Her throat closed around the words.

"You took her off life support?" he inquired gently.

"Not right away. Jase fought it. He fought until she began to have complications." She took a big jagged breath. "Afterward, his guilt and grief and rage consumed him. We wound up in limbo—unable to go back, but not able to move forward, either." She wiped away a tear, then looked at him. "I'm sorry I kept you in the dark. You've been nothing but wonderful, and I hate that you were blindsided tonight. My only excuse is that in my mind, the private grief kept Sydney alive in some way. Does that make any sense at all?"

"I can't pretend to understand it the way you do, but yeah. I guess it makes sense." He reached for her hands, holding them between his own. Willa could feel their wonderful heat warming her fingers. "I wish I could have comforted you. I wish I'd known your daughter."

Her eyes stung. "Me, too. On both counts."

"So it's really over between you and Jase?"

"It is." Now that she'd given him the facts and an apology, she wanted to tell him what she'd planned to say before Jase's arrival, but her nerves skyrocketed. With her heart flopping like a flounder in her chest, she looked into his eyes. "I'm ready to move forward now. With you."

Chapter Fourteen

Letting go of her hands, Derek leaned back, raising his face to the ceiling and exhaling a breath he seemed to have been holding for ages. Without looking at her, he put a hand on her thigh, squeezed and said, "Wait here." Then he rose and crossed to the coat tree in his entry.

Willa sat, baffled. Had she blown it? Stretched his patience to the snapping point? Waited too long to realize she wanted to realize her feelings ran deeper than those of a mere lover or friend?

On pins and needles, she watched him root through a pocket in his leather jacket. When he found what he wanted, he returned to her. Clearing his throat, he sat.

"I knew you'd lost someone. I saw the books on your front porch, the ones about grief. But I never dreamed you'd lost a child." He met her eyes. "You humble me. I don't mean that lightly, and I'm not patronizing you. There's not a doubt in my mind that you were an amazing mother to Sydney, because I've seen you with Gilberto. You're a natural."

Willa's heart beat in an erratic rhythm. Derek was unusually nervous.

"The thing is," he continued, "I knew from the beginning, from the time you first came to work for Izzy, that you were special. Loving and good in a way that didn't jive with the distance you were keeping. I told myself not to stalk you. I mean, if you weren't interested then how warped was it to keep pursuing you? But my gut said you were the one."

"Derek, I think… I… I should—"

"No, let me say this. It's what I meant to say when I got to your house tonight." His elbows were on his knees, his head turned toward her, his expression as open and vulnerable as she'd ever seen. "You're the love I've waited for. The past two weeks, while we were helping Gilberto with the play and couldn't even squeeze in a real date—they've been the most mundane, wonderful weeks of my life."

He looked down at his hands. Concentrating on his face, Willa had neglected to look at the item he held. Now she noticed it. *Oh. Oh, my. Oh, no.*

"I planned to do this earlier." Turning over his hand, he revealed a small, sapphire-blue velvet box.

Willa felt as if she were in a dream, the kind in which everything moved in slow motion, and you couldn't react quickly enough no matter how hard you tried.

"I love you, Willa. I don't want to waste another minute living without you. Whatever life brings, I want to be by your side." He opened the box. An absolutely stunning ruby-and-diamond ring glowed in its velvet bed. "The ruby reminds me of you. Unique, rare." The first genuine smile of the evening lit his face. "And, it goes real well with your hair."

Slipping from the sofa to the floor, with one knee bent, Derek asked humbly, "Will you marry me?"

"Oh, Derek." She reached for his hands, not the ring. Tears sprang to her eyes. "When I said I want to move forward, I… I meant it, but…in a relationship that's open-ended. I want to be there for you, too, but as a…a…" She struggled to find the right word. "A girlfriend." Derek's brows swooped abruptly. "A steady girlfriend," she assured, but she could tell by his expression that she was making it worse. The intensity of his stare unnerved her even more.

Silence as heavy as an anvil fell onto the conversation.

Slowly, Derek raised himself to the sofa. He snapped the ring box shut and dropped it on the table in front of them. Elbows on his knees, he put his head in his hands and spoke with great care. "I can see that after what you've been through, it would be hard to commit again. But I'm not Jase. I'll never walk away."

"That's not what this is about—"

"Of course it is," he insisted. "If you'd had someone to help you get through the pain—"

"It would have helped, yes, but it wouldn't change my mind about today. It was wonderful with Syd, but—" Anguish clogged her throat. "I don't want children of my own again, Derek. I just can't do it."

"You're still grieving. You don't know how you'll feel in time."

"I know how I *don't* want to feel again. It's been two years. You have to accept what I'm telling you."

"But you could be a girlfriend," he said, making her wince at the mocking tone. "So, if it was just me, you'd consider marriage?"

Willa had a hard time meeting his gaze. "I don't know how you did it," she said, "but you managed to break through every rational reason I ever had not to fall in love again." She shook her head rapidly. "I'm botching this so badly. I'm sorry. I know how much you want to be a father. The thing is, you *are* one. You and Gilberto are a package deal. I know how much having him here means to you. I do, and I'm happy for you. I just can't risk—" She blinked at the welling tears and fanned at the sudden heat in her cheeks with her fingertips. "I won't risk feeling that kind of pain again."

"And you think being a girlfriend will keep you safe?"

She felt like an idiot when he put it that way. "Maybe not completely, but…"

The tension in the air crackled to an uncomfortable level. "But as a girlfriend, you could walk away if you felt yourself getting in too deep. Right?" he demanded harshly then raised a hand before she could respond. "Never mind, I've heard enough." He stood and took a step back.

"I'm sorry."

"You said that."

Willa shook her head. She really was an idiot. It was over. Why hadn't she accepted the fact before she'd come here tonight? It had been selfish to assume she could chop her affections into carefully controlled bits, like a dieter trying to make a chocolate bar last as long as possible. Why would anyone be satisfied with that? Why should he?

Clasping her hands beneath her chin, she said, "I'm so sorry—okay, I know, you've heard that already. I don't know what to say except… I have to know my limits."

He swung around, his expression filled with disbelief. "That's the coward's way of saying you're still running away. Like Jase did."

"That's unfair! Jase had started drinking," Willa argued, feeling defensive now. "He was actually trying to protect me by leaving!"

"No, Willa. Jase was protecting *himself.* He ran away from the reality that life dishes out crap sometimes, and it's up to us to turn the crap into something decent. Something meaningful, even if we wouldn't choose it for ourselves in a million years. But you don't run away."

Standing now, Willa faced off with him. "You don't understand. You can't possibly understand."

Striding forward, Derek grasped her upper arms. "I know I love you. I know we should be together. Not only when it's easy and not just for a while. Forever. For better, for worse."

"Derek." Willa groaned with frustration. "You don't know what you're talking about. You don't! Don't tell me about forever."

"You're right. I've never lost a child. I don't know what that's like, not at all. But I know one thing—" he paused and took a deep breath "—I want a woman to love and a house full of kids to share that love with. I want pets and chaos and the whole messy works. I want it with you. And I believe, deep down, if you'd let yourself, you'd want that again, too."

No. Just...no. Though she wanted to explain, there were no more words. She couldn't do it again, and it was beyond her at the moment to make him understand.

No matter. He obviously read it in her face.

A log fell in the fireplace, sending a shower of sparks up the chimney as Derek scooped the ring box off the table and looked down at it. Captain's head swiveled toward them before he yawned noisily.

Derek bobbed his head once. "Okay."

Her chin wobbled miserably. "I'm—"

She stopped herself, but he knew what she was about to say and raised his eyes to hers. "No. If you were really sorry, you wouldn't be doing this."

She had no retort.

Derek shrugged. "Well, I guess this is it." He moved toward the foyer.

Wordlessly, Willa followed.

"Good night, Willa," he said, holding open the door.

She nodded, not trusting herself to push words through the new spate of grief that rose like a tidal wave.

Frigid air stung her lungs as she stepped onto his front porch. The click of the door behind her seemed as final as any sound she had ever heard.

Two nights later, Willa was wide awake and staring morosely at the shadowed ceiling above her bed when the phone rang. Yellow light pooled as she turned on her bedside lamp then searched the nightstand for her cell. DEREK, the screen read.

Pushing herself up against the headboard, she held her breath. They hadn't spoken or seen each other since he'd closed the door on the night he'd proposed. She'd moved like a zombie through the past two days, the grief she'd tried to avoid front and center no matter what she was doing. Now merely seeing his name on caller ID filled her with adrenaline. Had he changed his mind about insisting on marriage? Was he phoning to say he wanted to try being in an open-ended relationship after all?

Did it matter?

Since she'd left his house, Willa had become more convinced with each passing minute that it had been ludicrous to believe she could be Derek's "girlfriend" and still maintain a safe distance from Gilberto. Or, a safe distance from him, for that matter. Her mind and emotions were already in turmoil. Imagine if they'd been in a long standing relationship and *then* broke up. Or if they were together, in love, and he was killed on the job, God forbid. The very thought made her feel so sick, she thought she might throw up. What had she been thinking, getting involved with someone in his line of work?

While she fretted, the phone stopped ringing. Before she could decide whether she was relieved or disappointed, it started in again, and this time she checked the clock: 1:18 a.m. Emotionally and physically drained, she wondered whether she had enough energy to tackle another charged conversation.

Biting the inside of her lip, she gazed at the small screen. Curiosity was seductive.

She took the call.

"Hi," she murmured, hunkering back against her pillow and pulling the covers up around her shoulders.

"Willa?"

Instantly, her heart slammed into her throat. Once before, she'd answered a call in which she'd heard the same note of urgency when the caller spoke her name. Sitting straight up, she clutched the phone in a death grip. "What happened?"

"I'm sorry if I woke you up."

"Derek, what's wrong?"

"Gilberto is gone."

"What do you mean, gone?"

"I went into his room to check on him about an hour ago, and he wasn't in his bed."

She tried to swallow, but her throat felt like sandpaper. "Did he run away?"

"I don't know." It sounded as if Derek was pacing as he talked. "I don't know why he would. We've been doing great."

"You looked all over the house and grounds?"

"I searched every corner and called his name till I was

hoarse. Look, the reason I called is I thought maybe he'd hitched a ride to town and somehow made it to your place?"

"No and if he had, I'd have called, immediately."

She could tell he was grasping at straws. Head swimming, Willa jumped into a pair of jeans. "Where are you now?"

"I'm in my squad car. Over in Roddy's old neighborhood. I've got the entire force out looking for Gilberto, and we've put out an Amber Alert and an APB."

"Do you really think Roddy could have something to do with this?"

"I don't know. I have to explore every possibility."

"Of course. Does Roddy know where you live?"

"I don't know. Possibly. But Captain didn't bark, and he always lets me know when someone drives up."

"If Roddy did come back, do you think Gilberto went with him willingly?" The alternative made her blood freeze.

"I'm not sure. I didn't give enough consideration to the family bond." Remorse warred with the panic in his tone. "There've been so many changes for the poor kid. What the hell was I thinking, expecting everyone to move on from their pasts because I said so? I've been so damn blind—"

"No. Stop." Willa interrupted the self-condemning rant. "Derek, that boy loves you. He wants to live with *you*, not Roddy. He told me that several times when we were working on his costume for the school play. Whatever is going on, it has nothing to do with him feeling pressured to let go of his previous life. If he left with Roddy, it's because of divided loyalties, not because he wasn't happy where he was."

Derek fell silent, and she could tell he was pondering her words. Unfortunately, Gilberto was not with her.

"He's not here," she said.

"Damn it." Derek's worry and frustration were tangible. "Hang on."

In the background, Willa could hear him communicating on his radio. The muffled conversation made it clear that no one had seen Gilberto yet. When Derek came back on the line he said, "Look, I'm going to let you go so that I can focus here."

"Oh. Okay, right. Of course." She hated the idea of letting him go. "Just one more quick question. Did he take anything with him?"

"His backpack. And I'm pretty sure he had that Daniel Boone outfit you made him. I don't know what else." His radio squawked, and Russell began to relay some information. "I've gotta go."

"Let me know the second you hear anything," Willa said right before he hung up.

She sat on the edge of the bed. Her gut told her Roddy had not come back, but why would Gilberto run away? Something had to have happened. Something he couldn't cope with. But what? And, where would he have run if he was feeling some kind of emotional turmoil?

Her mind moved so fast she was breathless. And, why on earth would he have taken his costume? Unless…

She remembered the hike they'd taken in the days just prior to the history play. They'd driven out to a heavily forested area of a national park near the Long River called Winter Forks to get the feel of pioneer life. And to gather the sticks he needed to make his bow and arrow set.

"I could live out here," the boy had boasted. "I could use my bow and arrow to hunt rabbits. I'd build a fire to cook and keep warm. And I could build a lean-to right over there. It wouldn't be that hard."

She'd thought his bluster was endearing at the time, but now? Could he have been serious? And if he was, could he have gone back to the spot under the fallen tree he'd insisted would be the best place to set up camp? It was about two miles past Derek's place. He could have made it out there in under an hour, even in the dark.

Dear God. Don't let him get hit on the road.

A feeling deep in her gut urged her to head in that direction. Without further consideration, her feet were in motion. Quickly she found a backpack then put some leftover pizza in the microwave. While it was heating, she grabbed the blanket she kept hanging by the radiator and stuffed it into another bag. Once in the car, she tucked everything under the heating vent to keep it all warm.

Within minutes, she was backing out of the driveway, but stopped before she pulled out onto the street. Reaching for her cell phone, she texted Derek.

Heading to Winter Forks to search. Long shot. Will let you know ASAP if I find him.

During the seemingly interminable drive, turmoil over Gilberto's safety took on a life of its own. If anything happened to him, she knew Derek would never forgive himself.

Anxiety threatened to give way to panic and Willa had to fight to control her rapid breathing as she found the correct cutoff. Gravel crunched under her tires as she flipped her headlights on high beam and slowly worked her way down the crude forest access road. Trees cast long, eerie shadows and Winter Forks looked so very different than it had in broad daylight. Gaze roving from one side of the road to the other, Willa searched the woods for any sign of a young Daniel Boone making a campfire. Eventually, the spot she'd parked in the last time came in to view and she pulled over and cut the engine.

Please, God, don't let this be a wild goose chase. Or, if it is, let Derek find Gilberto right now. Right now!

Shoving her keys and cell phone into her backpack, she grabbed everything she'd brought with her, locked her doors, clicked on her flashlight and strode down the formidable forest trail, rage beginning to replace the fear that wanted to consume her.

This is not happening again. Nothing bad was going to happen to Gilberto. *I will not allow it.*

With a mother's intuition, she followed the path her heart told her to take.

Chapter Fifteen

It had to be close to freezing. Gilberto had complained that his Daniel Boone coat was too warm. Now Willa was grateful she'd ignored his protest. In the back of her mind, she could hear the echo of his young voice as they'd explored this trail the first time. *I could live out here, all by myself. I wouldn't be scared. Daniel Boone did it. I could, too.*

"All alone?" Willa had asked. "I think people need other people to live with."

"You don't," the boy had pointed out. "And you're not scared of anything."

How ironic that at this very moment her rage was underscored by the terror of losing Gilberto before she ever had a chance to tell him how much she loved him.

In the distance, she heard the sound of Long River rushing over a ravine filled with boulders. A coyote set up an alarm that was repeated across several hilltops, while, closer by, an owl hooted. The trail they'd taken several weeks ago was difficult to make out in the dim beam of her flashlight, but she forged on.

"Gilberto?" she shouted, swiveling the light from right to left. "Gilberto? Are you out here? If you are, please answer me!" She paused to listen. Nothing.

They'd hiked for quite a while that day, so she probably had another quarter mile to go? Maybe he couldn't hear her yet. "Gilberto?" she repeated every twenty paces.

Finally, she reached the spot where Gilberto had declared he'd easily forge the life of a pioneer, but there was no sign of him. "Gilberto!"

Battling back another wave of panic, Willa was about to admit her intuition had mislead her when she spied a backpack. Her heart lurched. It was his.

But where was he? "'Berto, answer me, please!" Heading more deeply into the woods, Willa continued to call his name. She was nearly at the riverbank when she heard a whimpering sound up ahead.

As she stumbled along the path, Willa's light illuminated the outline of a boy, shaking in his hiking boots.

"Gilberto? Oh, thank God!" She ran to his side. "Are you alright? Are you hurt, honey?"

When he didn't immediately answer, she followed the direction of his gaze with the beam of her flashlight.

Her relief proved short-lived. Up ahead about thirty feet, a black bear stood, head swaying as he stared into the light. *Dear Lord.* Spring was on the horizon, and hibernation must have given way to hunger. Frantically, Willa tried to remember everything she knew about bears.

Nothing.

What was it the old-timers in town said? What was that one rhyme? If it's black, attack. If it's brown, lie down? It was hard to tell what the hell color this guy was, but she knew black bears were more common in this area. Why had she left her pepper spray in the glove box?

"I… I think he wants my sandwich," Gilberto managed to croak.

Willa wasn't sure it was a sandwich the bear wanted, but she wasn't going to quibble.

"Sweetie." She pushed the fear-frozen boy behind her. "Yeah, he's probably hungry, huh? So, I have some pizza in my backpack, and we're going to slowly take it out and toss it at him, okay? And then we're gonna run like crazy." In her peripheral vision, she could see Gilberto nodding. "Good. Now, just unzip my—"

Their slight movements seemed to encourage the bear to rise up on its haunches and emit a noise that smacked of his impatience.

"Change of plans," Willa whispered, slipping the backpack off her shoulders. With strength worthy of a Scots log thrower, she hurled it at the huge animal. She grabbed Gilberto by the hand. *"Run!"* she screamed.

Behind them, the bear wasted no time tearing into the pack and locating the pizza. Unfortunately, the animal was now also in possession of Willa's cell phone and car keys, but she would worry about that later. Much later. After she and Gilberto thrashed their way through this blasted forest and out to the main road.

By the time they reached her car, Willa's breath was coming in knife-like jabs. Bent over, Gilberto sucked in heaving lungfuls of air. Willa didn't pause long, however, before she pulled the boy into her arms.

"What are you doing out here? You scared me half to death. Don't you ever run away like that again, do you hear me?" She pushed him far enough away to scan his head and body, checking to be sure every finger and toe was intact, the way one would with a newborn. Then she swept him against her heart and held on, whispering fiercely in his ear. "I love you. I couldn't stand it if anything happened to you."

Gilberto cried, clutching her as they stood outside her parked car and rocked together. When the flood of emotion subsided some, Willa thought of the blankets she'd carried in the second bag and realized she'd dropped it somewhere on their flight through the woods.

"I think the bear ate my car keys," Willa said, "and my phone." Attempting to add a little levity to the situation for Gilberto's sake. "We're sort of on our own at the moment. But that's okay. I told Derek where I thought you might be and knowing him, he's going to find us real soon. We just need to keep moving," she told the teeth-chattering boy, "to keep warm. And, to get back to the main road, okay?"

He nodded in assent and meekly followed her lead.

Willa kept the pace at a good clip, not only to create warmth, but also because the idea that there were other predators lurking in the shadows had her spooked. When she saw the highway up ahead, she knew they had two miles to Derek's house.

"How are you doing?" she asked her companion, who still looked shaken.

"Good."

"Good. So. Want to tell me what made you leave your warm, comfortable bed in the middle of the night and move in with the bears?"

Misery filled his voice. "I heard what you and Derek were talking about the other night."

She swallowed. "You did? I must have woken you up, huh?"

"Nah. I was already awake. But I knew something was wrong with you guys, so I listened in." He shrugged and shot a guilty glance up at her.

Hot shame filled her belly. What had the conversation sounded like to his young ears? She'd told Derek she didn't want to love a child again.

"You left because of what I said?"

"Uh, uh. I left because Derek was really sad, and I knew he wouldn't feel better until you married him, and you wouldn't marry him until I left."

"No!" She swept him into her arms. "No, that's not right. Oh, buddy, listen to me." Holding him at arm's length, she stared hard at his face in the moonlight. "If you were eavesdropping, you know I had a daughter. And that I lost her. I want to talk to you more about that when we're not freezing half to death, but for now, you need to understand that I didn't turn down Derek's proposal because of you. I turned it down because of me. Because I'm scared of being married again."

Gilberto's brows were pulled tightly together. "How come?"

She shook her head. "I'm scared of lots of things, I guess. And that's something I have to work on. But it's my problem, not yours. Not Derek's, either. He's...he's great, and he loves you. Do you know he'd go nuts if anything happened to you? So you can't ever run away like that again, right?"

A tear slipped silently down his smooth cheek. His lower lip trembled as he wiped the moisture from his eyes and nodded, and she hugged him again, squeezing so tightly, he eventually wriggled to be free.

Before they could say any more, the sound of an engine slowing and tires turning onto the access road was followed by the blinding glare of headlights on high beams. Red and blue lights swirled from the approaching car and bounced off the treetops.

Derek!

Awash in the lights, Willa and Gilberto stood in the middle of the road as the squad car sped up beside them and skidded to a stop. Derek leaped from the car, pulling Gilberto into his arms. There were tears in Derek's voice as he reached for Willa, too, and included her in the embrace. "Thank you. Thank you so much," he murmured against the top of her head.

Willa nodded. They hung on to each other as if each was afraid one of the others might disappear. She buried her face against Derek's chest.

The relief that should have washed away all else got dammed up inside Willa. Gilberto had run away, because of her. The beautiful boy huddled between them had believed he was nothing more than a stumbling block on the road to her romance with Derek, and it was her fault. As for the man who'd offered to love her through thick and thin…

A shudder ran through her. Her own aching heart had led her to break two more, and that wasn't okay. It wasn't okay at all.

It was almost 3:00 a.m. when they all trooped in through the front door, and four by the time Derek had Gilberto tucked into bed. When he finally came downstairs and into the kitchen, Willa could see the exhaustion in his eyes.

"Something smells good," he said.

The closeness they'd shared in the forest had yielded to lingering uncertainty. She gestured toward the frying pan on the stove. "Turkey sausage and scrambled eggs. I thought you'd be hungry."

"I am."

"Have a seat. It's ready."

He complied and, running a hand over his face, told her, "Gilberto overheard our conversation."

"I know." Serving up the sausage and eggs, she arranged triangles of buttered toast on the edge of the plate. "He was telling me that right before you arrived." Legs rubbery, Willa set the food down in front of Derek and sank heavily into the chair across from him. "I blew it."

Reaching across the table, he placed a comforting hand on her arm. "He's a kid. He couldn't understand the context."

"Neither did I, apparently. Everything was clear in my mind until you phoned to say he was gone. And then when I saw him in front of that bear—"

"None of that was your fault."

She shot him the kind of *puh-lease* look that Gilberto was mastering. "He wanted us to have a chance at a relationship. I'd say that was more mature than I was being."

The hint of a smile appeared on Derek's face. "As crazy and misguided and dangerous as it was for him to run away, the sacrifice he made was probably the nicest thing anyone has ever done for me."

"Children are like that. You think all they care about is themselves, and then they surprise you by how much they notice. How much they're willing to give to make you happy."

"Yeah." He looked down at his hands, folded now on the counter. "You were right. Gilberto is mine. I couldn't lose him now."

Willa nodded, mentally comparing the two great romantic loves of her life, Jase and Derek. They were both wonderful men, but fundamentally so different.

Jase turned in on himself during a crisis, withdrawing from her so totally it was as if they were in separate rooms even as they shared a bed. Derek's care was as reliable as the tide.

Suddenly, he looked up. "I didn't think this all the way through. You're locked out of your house, aren't you?"

Willa blinked. She hadn't thought of that, either. "Yes. I guess I am."

"Got a spare key hidden somewhere?"

"No."

"Good. It's not safe." He eyed her steadily. "Stay."

A simple invitation, yet one that sparked myriad possibilities.

"I want to," she whispered.

"Good. I'll make up the guest room for you."

"No. You've got to be exhausted. I can—"

"You can decide not to argue." He forked up a bite of scrambled eggs. "I'll draw you a bath, too."

"You certainly will not!"

Sternly, he arched a brow. "Arguing at four in the morning is exhausting."

That stopped her. Besides, a bath did sound heavenly. "Thank you."

"You're welcome." He tried the sausage then added, "Just because I'm being hospitable, it doesn't mean I'm not still angry you went off into the woods by yourself."

"I couldn't *not* go."

"Yes. You could have wai—"

"No." She shook her head when he tried to rebut. "Mothers don't wait." Leaning forward, she beseeched him with her eyes. "I think I've finally figured out some things."

The hand holding the fork slowly lowered. "I'm listening."

"When Gilberto and I were the woods, the only thing that mattered was getting back to you. I knew you were out there looking for us, that you wouldn't stop looking until you found us, and I realized you were right. Believing in the person you love, being one hundred percent certain you can count on him…it changes things. It makes you go the distance."

She reached for Derek's hands. He was so still, she knew he was listening to every word. "Before I met you, I didn't think it was right to let go of my grief. I thought if I let go all the way, it would be a betrayal."

"I'm not going to ask you to let go, Willa."

With her fingers curled around his, she could feel his reserve. He didn't pull away, but he wasn't holding onto her, either. Not the way he had in the past.

"You were right," he acknowledged. "There's no way I can understand what you went through. After tonight, though, I think I get it a little bit more. I was terrified I might lose the one thing that finally means more to me than my own life."

"Gilberto." Grateful on his behalf, tears filled her eyes, and she nodded. "That's exactly how a father feels."

"Yeah. I do feel like his father. But I don't mean only Gilberto." Fiercely, his gaze bore into hers. "First day I saw you in the deli, I started wanting something I'd told myself a long time ago didn't exist. I wasn't even eighteen when I figured believing in 'forever' was bull, and if people couldn't see that, then they were fools asking to be kicked in the teeth. All I knew about love was how to turn my back on it before it turned its back on me." Pulling one of his hands free of hers, he rubbed his forehead. "When I saw you with Jase, I was angry. I was stinking-ugly angrier than I had any right to be. I know you had what you wanted with him and Sydney. I know that was supposed to be your happily-ever-after. It should have been."

Her heart squeezed hard. For a second she almost wished for Derek's sake that he'd fallen for someone with a simpler past.

Releasing his other hand, she came around the counter to stand in front of him, eye-to-eye with him seated on the stool. "Listen to me, Sheriff. You are not my consolation prize. Do you understand? I have never—not for a second—thought, 'Well I already had the best in life, so now I'm willing to settle.' You're a gift."

Gently, she brushed the thick black hair that had fallen over his forehead. "The thing is, when reality blows happily-ever-after out of the water, you begin to think true joy is a gift with someone else's name on it. So when a man comes along—a very, very good man—and he reminds you that your heart may be broken, but it hasn't stopped beating…you don't necessarily know what to do with that. I can't believe you were so patient with me for so long, but I sure am grateful." She rubbed an index finger over his puckered brow, trying to erase the frown line. "If you're willing to give me another chance, I promise it'll be the last one I'll ever need."

Tension radiated from every muscle in his strong, hyperalert body. His expression was impossible to read, and Willa felt panic begin to stir.

"Tell me what you're thinking," she urged.

Slowly, he nodded. "Okay. I'm thinking that you'd better be planning to make an honest man out of me. Because if you're still talking about an affair—"

She threw her arms around his neck before he could finish the sentence. "I'm talking about locking you up and throwing away the key, Sheriff. As far as I'm concerned, this is for good."

Derek half growled, half grinned his response. "Oh, it's going to be a whole lot better than good." Pulling her onto his lap, he went for a soul-searing kiss.

When they came up for air, Willa felt dizzy. "Wow. You are a mighty fine kisser."

Pressing those magical lips into a tight line, he rued, "Darn it. I knew this was going to happen."

"What?"

"Now you only want me because of my amazing sexual prowess."

Even though he was kidding, she figured laughing *very* hard might hurt his feelings. It was nice, though, it was very nice, to feel as if her heart were light enough to float. She patted his chest. "Don't sell yourself short. You're a man of many layers, and I plan to explore all of them."

A smile of unbridled joy stretched across his face. "Better get started then." After another incendiary kiss, he pulled back to study her, using his thumb to trace her lips with a touch as gentle as summer rain. "We'll take this happily-ever-after thing one day at a time," he promised.

If Thunder Ridge could talk, it would have sounded just like Derek then. Powerful, reassuring, able to shelter the ones it loved from the harshest of life's elements. The perfect haven for a woman truly ready to start living again.

"Should we wake Gilberto?" she asked as she snuggled against Derek. "Tell him we kissed and made up?"

"Nah, let the kid sleep. I want him to be wide awake tomorrow when we propose to you."

This time, her heart leaped with excitement, not fear. Raising her head, she looked at him, adoring the crook of his dark brow. "It's going to take two of you to do the job, huh?"

"Absolutely. Like you said, we're a package deal." Reaching for her hand, he raised it, kissing her temporarily bare ring finger. "For better, for worse, from this day forward. I love you with all my heart, Willa Holmes."

"From this day forward," she agreed in a whisper, nodding. "I love you, too, Derek Neel."

If it were possible, Willa thought, she'd cling to this golden feeling and never let it go.

Slipping her arms all the way around Derek's waist,

she murmured, "You can kiss me again, Sheriff, whenever you're ready."

She didn't have long to wait.

Through the windows behind them, the sky began to glow pink as the sun rose on two people ready to face the beautiful, uncertain future together.

Epilogue

"What do you think?" Willa asked the marmalade tabby she used to feed in the park before work every morning. Growing courageous, he'd followed her to the bakery one day and had chosen not to leave. Together, they'd decided his name should be Harold and struck a bargain: he agreed to remain on the ground unless someone picked him up, and she promised to bring him whitefish and lox scraps from the deli as a reward. At night, he slept at her place.

"It's good, isn't it?" she said, scooping the cat up so he'd have a better view of the cake she'd been decorating for the past several hours. Instantly, he favored her with his bass, outboard-motor purr. "Really? You think I'm a genius? Nah, you're just saying that." He rubbed his nose against her chin. "All right, if you insist." In truth, she was one hundred percent satisfied with her efforts.

A knock on Something Sweet's front door startled her. The bakery was closed, chair seats resting on tabletops and only the work lights on. The wildflower-filled spring they'd all enjoyed this year was yielding already to verdant summer with longer days, but for now the sun still set before nine, and it was a full hour past that. She certainly wasn't expecting anyone.

Willa couldn't see the person standing outside the door until she was more than halfway there. When recognition hit, she gave a happy gasp. Setting Harold on the floor, she raced to the front, fishing the key for the dead bolt out of her pocket. "What are you doing here?" she asked as she opened the door, throwing her arms around Derek's neck. "I thought you and 'Berto were enjoying your last night as bachelors. Is he with you?" Leaning to the right, she tried to see around her husband-to-be.

Derek kissed her soundly on the lips before answering. "Izzy, Nate and Eli invited him to go bowling. The question is, what are you doing at work this late, bride-to-be? You're supposed to be home, getting your beauty sleep."

"I'm busy." Yesterday, he'd made her promise she wouldn't work all day before their wedding. Now she gave him a kiss that she intended to be thoroughly distracting, then said, "If you're all alone tonight, why aren't you home, dreaming about me?"

With a hand on her lower back, he pressed her closer. "I do that every day, with my eyes wide open."

"That deserves another kiss." Grinning, she delivered it. "Okay, now go," she ordered, making shooing motions.

"I just got here," he protested. "When you weren't at your place, I figured you were working on our cake, despite giving me your word you'd quit at six."

"I said seven."

"It's almost ten. Where's the cake? Let's see it."

"Before the wedding?" She crossed her arms. "Nope."

Tomorrow she was marrying Sheriff Derek Neel in a

wedding that had started out small and blossomed into a come-one, come-all bash. Derek was, after all, a beloved community member. So was Gilberto.

And so was she.

After more than two years of wandering, Willa had found her Promised Land right here in Thunder Ridge. That merited a rock-star cake.

"Time for you to scoot," she told him.

Derek adopted the stubborn expression she was coming to know quite well. "Izzy told me I couldn't see you in your wedding dress. She didn't say anything about the cake. Lead on."

After a moment's thought, Willa shrugged. It might be better for him to see it before their guests. She had, after all, planned a surprise that was exclusively for Derek.

Preceding him to the kitchen, she made a sweeping "ta-da" gesture.

"That's incredible," he said as he gazed in obvious appreciation at the six-tiered, white-chocolate, buttercream-covered pièce de résistance she had draped with the sugar flowers, leaves and branches she'd been making in her spare time for the past few weeks. "Wait a minute, is that…"

Willa watched closely as he peered intently at the top tier, the one intended to be their anniversary layer.

Derek began to laugh, a robust, pleasure-filled sound that invariably made her feel as if the sun was shining straight into her heart.

"Yes, indeed," she confirmed. "Our anniversary cake s a chocolate chip babka. It worked wonders for Mr. and rs. Wittenberg. She isn't here in the mornings anymore, know. She and Mr. W 'sleep in' now." Willa winked ly. "So, I figured a year from now on our first anrsary, when the flames of passion have died down…"

"I'll need a chocolate chip babka to bring them back?"

"Well, you're not getting any younger. Remember what Mrs. W said. According to the Food Network, breakfast treats can be a potent aphrodisiac."

"Is that so?" Sweeping her into a kiss so hot it could have set the bakery on fire, Derek took his sweet time making her eat her words. "Still worried?" he murmured finally, against her lips.

"Mmm, not so much." Willa felt decidedly, deliciously dazed as Derek released her.

"I brought you something," he said, brandishing a small square box she hadn't even noticed he was carrying. Opening it himself, he removed a few tissue-wrapped items and handed them to her. When she uncovered three ceramic figurines, she laughed with sheer pleasure. "Cake toppers!"

"Yep," he agreed as she held up a miniature Sheriff Neel, a baker Willa and a little Gilberto.

"They're wonderful. I love them." Moving to the cake, she arranged the little figures in the buttercream, one tier below the dome-shaped anniversary babka. "Now it's perfect."

"Not yet." Derek withdrew another item from the box.

This time when Willa unwrapped the gift, she gave a sharp intake of breath. No words could get past the sudden tightness in her throat.

"Is it okay?" Derek asked, his voice betraying his sudden nerves. "You've been so happy lately, and I don't want to make you sad—that's the last thing I want—but it's important, and… I hope it's okay," he concluded, his habitua[illegible] strength softened by concern.

"More than okay," she whispered. "So much more[illegible] okay." Reverently touching the lovely ceramic cre[illegible] she looked up at him. "But how—?"